The White Buffalo

By Alan Gold

The White Buffalo
By Alan Gold
©2012 by Alan Gold

ISBN 1-893793-20-6

Fifth Leg Publishing
www.fifthleg.com

Chapter 1
The White Buffalo

L innie stared at the ceiling and wondered what had awakened her. Instead of the calming silence that may have been her favorite part of West Texas nights, something was humming at such a deep pitch she couldn't tell whether she heard it, or just felt it through the bedsprings.

"Coy—" she started, turning her head on the pillow before she remembered that Coy hadn't made it back from Tulia last night. He was supposed to be home by eleven, but she watched the clock flip over to four-thirteen.

She could just see him pulling up in broad daylight, slamming the door of the pickup because he was too tired to eat and too hungry to sleep. "Things always take a little longer than you'd think," he'll say. "You can't hurry waiting."

Nobody ever warned her that someone you love and who isn't even there can make you so mad you can't sleep. Why is it that you can wake up in the middle of the night and see things with perfect clarity, but when the alarm goes off in the morning your mind is like so much oatmeal?

The clanging that woke her rang out again. She bolted from the bed, stubbed her toe, stumbled into the living room and split the blinds. The commotion outside had activated the security light. Linnie's breath caught in her throat.

The buffalo had crashed through the cyclone fence, kicked the petunias to kingdom come, and was rolling in the neat, cropped grass of the front yard.

Linnie ran to the doorway and moaned, "Oh, Wanda, not here! Not now!"

She stepped on the porch and heard the deep rumbling sound again. She realized it was the mesh of the cyclone fence vibrating like a giant tuning fork.

Linnie dashed back inside and grabbed her robe and slippers. She threw the robe in the corner. This was going to be a boots-and-jeans job. She ran back to the porch, tucking a handful of shirt tail under her belt, then stopped. Use the phone!

She ducked back into the house and picked up the receiver. Who was she going to call? Coy was on the road somewhere. Doc Biffin was a horse vet. He didn't know any more about buffalo than frogs. Besides, everyone in the world- Biffin had figured Wanda had another month before the baby was due and that would give him time to study up on the subject. Who was it that said things take longer than you think?

Linnie moved closer to the buffalo and wondered what she could do to help. Wanda, half a ton of muscle, bone and fur thrashed and heaved in the damp grass. Her flanks swelled and collapsed. Her breath formed faint clouds in the cool air and Linnie didn't know what to do but watch in awe.

Coy trained cutting horses. Linnie thought that cutting was the most primal sport. A cutting horse separates one cow from the herd. Instinct tells the cow to go back to the herd, but the horse blocks it, matching every lunge and sprint. Coy spent as much time training riders not to interfere with the horse as he did polishing the horse's cutting techniques.

But now Linnie watched an even more primitive effort.

Linnie knew horses. She'd helped deliver a hundred foals. But she didn't know what to do with a buffalo. She couldn't even tell if things were going well in the harsh cone of light that spread over the yard.

She moved closer to Wanda and bent down warily as she caught the first glimpse of the baby. Linnie reached out to help and Wanda snorted.

"Coy," Linnie muttered, "you just wait until you get back. You just wait."

For Linnie, the ordeal blurred into a rhythm of pulling and cussing, waiting and praying, brushing the hair back from her forehead with a damp wrist. Minutes seemed like hours and she felt as tired as Wanda looked by the time she pulled the baby free.

The sun appeared like a fierce jewel over Wild Horse Bluff as Linnie bent over the baby buffalo. The West Texas plains, which had been old long before the first buffalo, looked like fire in the magic of the dawn.

Linnie watched with relief while Wanda licked her baby. She didn't even hear Coy drive up until the pickup door slammed.

"Sorry, hon, things always take a little longer than you'd think—" he started. Then he shouted, "Holy cow!" as he ran to her side.

"Coy Cooper, you don't have any idea how much trouble you're in now—"

"Linnie, that's a white buffalo."

"I'm the one who should tell you that. What I want to know is where you've been and who do you think you are, leaving me here alone at a time like this?"

"Linnie, buffalo are brown. There's never been a white buffalo before. Not for a hundred years anyway."

Coy threw his hat down so Linnie knew this was something important. She squinted at the baby, at Wanda, at Coy, and tears of relief flooded her eyes. "I thought it looked like that because it was a baby," she said.

Chapter 2
Buffalo Days

The sky had its thunder, the waters their rush and roar. But if the earth could claim a sound it would be the rumble of the buffalo across a distant plain, a rumble that welled up through your feet even before your ears sensed it.

It was the sound of life overtaking the planet. It was the song of a hundred thousand lungs breathing in unison, of muscle, sinew, bone and hair rushing ever onward.

In late summer the buffalo performed the greatest demonstration of the herding instinct that the world has ever known. On far-flung pastures, they paused in their grazing, cocked their heads and sniffed the wind, searching for a message that meant nothing to man. They stirred, restless, joining one to another, group to group, until their numbers passed all reckoning. A thousand pounds, fifteen hundred pounds or more apiece, they spilled over the horizon. As they loped, the herd needed four hours or more to pass a single point. A million pounding hooves churned the earth into a fine powder that rose like a messenger of the spirit.

For centuries, the tribes of man knew that the buffalo was as important as the sun itself for bringing life to the land. The great herds were the milk and honey of North America, sustaining man's soul as well as his stomach. The buffalo gave birth to legends of bravery. The sacrifice of mighty beasts was rewarded by the renewal of life.

The buffalo's flesh provided food. His skin provided clothes and housing. He gave man tools, vessels, even leisure because he was so readily available he required no long-term investment of time. To the Native American, the buffalo was not just symbolic of life, he was life.

In lean times, hunters might not see their perplexing quarry for days, but the signs were everywhere: in the maze of trails the buffalo tide had etched into the plains, in the rock-hard wallows, and in the trees where the bark had been scoured away to the full height of the beast.

Like a prehistoric interstate highway system, the buffalo's tracks led man over difficult terrain. They led him to water and to food—the buffalo himself. The buffalo's restless wandering gave the Indians who followed him their nomadic lifestyle, echoed in the westward urges of the Europeans who came later. The instinct that drove the buffalo together in a teeming celebration of life also set the stage for their destruction.

Like so many natural resources, the buffalo was squandered by the newcomers to the New World. The great beasts, which once covered the earth like a single robe, fell victim to greed and vanity. Their bones rose like mountains from the plains. They became the government's pawn in the Indian wars.

While the ordinary brown buffalo's abundance nearly condemned him because his life was so cheap, the white buffalo's extreme rarity put him in jeopardy. Seen as the leader of the herd, as a spiritual intermediary, the white buffalo conferred special powers on the man who killed it. Its value reached far beyond the material world, beyond the sustenance provided by its brethren. White buffalo were the stuff of legends, and of dreams.

Each tribe regarded the white buffalo in a different way and attached different rituals to it. The white buffalo tapped into the imagination, where it could fill a thousand roles and leave a different mark on each who saw it.

When European explorers tried to describe the creature they found in the New World, they compared it to the camel, lion, bull, mule and snake. Like beauty, the buffalo was in the eye of the beholder.

Chapter 3
The Way Things Used To Be

Kenny Rivers didn't hear anything the night the white buffalo was born because his house was down by the back road, on the other side of the cedar brake. The first thing he heard that morning was the tinny sound of Don't Fence Me In coming out of the radio.

He rubbed his eyes and ran his hand through his black hair, surprised by how long it had grown already. He'd always kept his hair short, but now he'd decided not to cut it until the Futurity. It symbolized his commitment to the event. Growing hair was kind of like training a horse; the daily changes were too small to see, but in the long run they could not be denied.

Kenny twisted the knob on the radio to find some young country. He never did understand why they always played that old stuff in the morning before a fellow was wide enough awake to defend himself.

By the time he'd downed a cup of instant coffee from the microwave and driven on up to the house, he could see that Coy was leaning against the pickup. One good thing about working for Coy was that you never had to worry about being chewed out if you were a few minutes late. The only thing Coy was never late for was feeding the horses. Horses have better clocks than we do, Coy always said. And they don't know or care about your plans and appointments. If breakfast is late, they get to worrying that it might never come.

"Didn't you say your grandpa's a Cherokee?" Coy asked Kenny before he even said, "Hey, morning!"

Kenny looked at him blankly for a moment. "Comanche, I think," he said. "Anyway, it's my grandma."

Coy nodded. "She ever tell you any buffalo stories?"

"What kind of buffalo stories?"

"Heck, I don't know." Coy rubbed the whiskers he hadn't had time to shave that morning. "That's why I'm asking. I thought maybe some buffalo stories got handed down from generation to generation." Coy looked at Kenny and raised his eyebrows. Sometimes it seemed like he could communicate with horses better than he could with people. Half the time a horse knew what you wanted even if you didn't know yourself.

"You mean like Great Buffalo Spirit met Elk and Deer in the Happy Hunting Ground? Maybe you should ask me about Santa Claus and the Easter Bunny," Kenny said, moving a pebble around in the dirt with the toe of his boot. "How about you?" He turned his best poker face to Coy. "Your grandma ever tell you any buffalo stories?"

"I reckon not, but my grandma was a Texan."

"So's both of mine," Kenny said. "But I hear you've got a yankee on your mama's side."

"The reason I asked, Chief Smartmouth, is Wanda had her baby last night."

"That's great!" Kenny lost his poker face.

"It's a girl," Coy said. "And it's white."

"I've never seen a white buffalo."

"I don't think much of anyone alive today has." Coy led him around to the front yard. "There weren't but a handful of them back when a buffalo herd could have covered Coyote County from corner to corner."

Kenny had spent most of his twenty-two years trying to bury the part of his heritage that made him stick out and feel awkward. He never gave much thought to his ancestry beyond the fact that being part Cherokee or Comanche or whatever made an impression on some girls he met. It didn't matter much to him, any more than it mattered to Coy that Coy's great grandfather had been an Appalachian moonshiner before he moved his trade to Texas. The only difference Kenny could see was that his legacy came along with bloody noses and bruised feelings as he grew up.

One day when they were six years old, Larry Skinner pushed him off the swing. When Kenny regained his feet, Larry slugged him in the stomach and said, "This one's for Custer."

It didn't seem fair to Kenny, who didn't feel like or want to be an Indian. Like every other kid at Buford Elementary School, his main ambition in life was to be a cowboy. Maybe the bullies inspired him to work harder than his friends at being a cowboy, and that's what drove him to be a top hand. Kenny figured that you made yourself what you wanted to be and your parents and their parents and their parents didn't make a whole lot of difference. Adam and Eve never showed up when you had work to do.

But as he and Coy rounded the corner of the house and saw Linnie leaning back on her elbows watching Wanda and the baby, he felt a catch in his throat.

"Hope," Linnie said over her shoulder.

"What?" asked Coy.

"I think we should call her 'Hope' because she's so new, because all of a sudden all kinds of things seem possible."

Neither of the men said anything, which wasn't unusual, so Linnie went on, "You know I was mad as hell at you for not being here to help me, Coy Cooper. But when she came out, I realized I didn't need you for that. I could do everything that needed to be done, if I had to."

Linnie sat up and wrapped her arms around her knees. She looked at Coy and went on, "Don't go hanging your head on me. You're good for a lot of things, but birthing buffaloes isn't one of them. You can tune my horse and you can fix my leaky faucet, but I'm going to be in charge when it comes to buffalo babies."

Linnie's smile stretched clear across the horizon. "I figure that's some kind of miracle," she said, "how something that hasn't even opened its own eyes yet can open your eyes for you."

Chapter 4
The Park Place Coyote

Years before Stubby Hitchins bought his first buffalo, his daddy used to tell him that big cars and smooth roads were the best thing that ever happened to West Texas.

"Only thing I like to see coming out of this country," B.K. Hitchins Sr. said, stabbing a cold cigar at the windshield, "is me.

"Just mile after mile of nothing a poor man would want to know about. You know why a minute here steals two minutes out of life?"

Stubby looked up at his father across the shiny new 1949 Oldsmobile's wide, plush seat. He shook his head, but his father didn't even glance in his direction. The man went on, clucking his tongue and shaking his own head, "The first minute you lose is the one you spend here trying to get out. The second minute is the one you spend later wondering what you ever did to make God send you to West Texas in the first place."

Stubby always took his daddy's lessons very seriously for two reasons. For one thing, there were so few of them that he figured they must be important. And for another thing, those lessons were just about the only times his daddy paid any kind of attention to him, so Stubby didn't want to miss out on any part.

Stubby knitted his brow. He turned the words over and over in his mind while he sucked on his lower lip like someone trying to pull the last drops out of a lemon, but it still didn't make much sense.

In the first place, although he was too young then to know the numbers, he had a pretty good idea that his daddy wasn't a poor man. After all, Stubby had seen plenty of old, brown photographs of his daddy with men with watch chains dangling across their vests, bankers and politicians, captains of industry—even Will Rogers and Bob Wills.

In the second place, it seemed simple to a kid like Stubby that you could use the first minute, the one where you were actually in West Texas, wondering why God put you there, and save that second minute for something more important later.

They'd driven several miles when Stubby finally asked, "Why?"

"Why what?" B.K. barked, making his son wince.

"I don't know." Stubby shrugged.

"Why don't you go ahead and play your game and let me think?"

Stubby spent a great deal of his childhood playing Monopoly in a brand new Oldsmobile while his father drove back and forth across West Texas. For all his cussing about the open country, it had given B.K. wealth and power. He was always setting off for a few days to visit one or another of his newspapers and it wasn't until Stubby was an adult himself that he realized his daddy had probably been trying to avoid Myrna as much as he was doing any sort of useful business on these trips.

Hat pins—each one representing a newspaper, and each color representing a certain level of circulation—studded the western half of the big Texas map back in B.K.'s office. It seemed like every week a man took Stubby out of school and sat him in the enormous leather chair outside B.K.'s door. By and by, B.K. called his son in, tapped one of the hat pins, and said, "Hey, buckaroo, let's go to Abilene," or Lubbock or Snyder or some other place that seemed to exist on the far rim of this great wasteland his daddy said he hated so much.

Sometimes those would be the only words Stubby would hear from his daddy until they reached their destination. On one trip, when B.K. got a little riled by the way his son kept kicking the front of the seat with his heels, he realized Stubby needed something to do to help fill in the miles.

B.K. custom ordered a Monopoly game for Stubby. A man he knew painted the board on a steel plate. Each of the markers, houses and hotels—everything except the dice—had a magnet in its base. The Chance and Opportunity cards fit into holders welded to the side of the board.

Before he learned the rules of the game, Stubby staged races around the board with the markers. He imagined the houses and hotels that he sprinkled across the middle of the board were ranches, and that the Scotch terrier marker was the coyote that preyed on them.

"Ow-ooo! Ow-ooo!" Stubby cried as he lumbered the dog through a stand of houses like Godzilla in Tokyo.

B.K. rose six inches off the seat and slammed on the brakes. "What's the matter with you, boy? That's not how you play Monopoly. I might as well have you jabbering away for five hundred miles as this."

Faced with his daddy's wrath, Stubby quickly learned the rules of the game. Day after day, he played himself for the Monopoly championship of the universe. While his peers plugged away at reading, writing, and arithmetic, and became aware of certain social graces back in the city, Stubby sharpened his negotiating skills and discovered how to wring the greatest value out of his capital.

While his classmates grew up to be doctors, plumbers, engineers, burglars and bureaucrats, Stubby grew up to be rich beyond calculation. When the reporter from Forbes asked about his net worth, Stubby shrugged and said, "After you reach a certain point, money is like life: by the time you've finished counting, it's gone and changed on you."

Not that B.K. "Stubby" Hitchins Jr. ever actually grew up in the ways most people understand growing up. In hindsight, the nickname his father had given him seemed prophetic. After the age of twelve, his body seemed determined to end up looking like a fire plug. And, because he spent his childhood trying to beat himself at Monopoly, and he later found that he could own just about anything he wanted, he never realized that he had missed out on certain lessons in life that his scrapping brethren cursed as their birthright.

Like a lot of kids, Stubby wanted to be a cowboy. He didn't turn out looking much like the Marlboro Man. And he patted the dust out of his jeans and grinned when he heard the Humpty Dumpty jokes at his first riding lessons as a young man.

But as an adult who thought success would make him less awkward and more popular, Stubby could afford to buy a little bay mare he named Money Honey which promised to be one of the greatest cutting horse prospects in the land. He could afford to give Coy Cooper generous terms for training his horses. And when Coy told him how buffalo were better in some ways than cows for teaching a horse the finer points of cutting, Stubby could afford to buy a whole herd of shaggy beasts to stock Coy's Double C Ranch out in Coyote County.

Stubby took good care of his people, partly because they worked better when he did, and partly because he just plain wanted them to like him. He gave them responsibility, he rewarded their achievements, and he urged them to be happy.

He'd diversified his father's publishing empire to the extent that nothing short of the end of civilization could put him in the poor house. And his personal stake was big enough that he never worried much about corporate takeovers or shareholder revolts.

And B.K. "Stubby" Hitchins Jr. would never have guessed in a million years that it might all fall apart because of a baby buffalo out in Coyote County.

Chapter 5
Midwife to a Miracle

Linnie Cooper was thirty-two years old. She had brown hair and intense brown eyes that Coy always said could melt a heart or burn down a corn field. She'd never seen a real, live horse until her sixteenth birthday, but she rode like she'd been born in the saddle.

And she couldn't help but believe in magic and miracles. She didn't have much choice when she saw them happen every day all around her. Sometimes, if you didn't catch yourself, you could almost start to take the wonderful things for granted.

When she was little, maybe ten, twelve years old, she'd dreamt and ached to see a horse some day, but she never would have imagined that she would ever see a live buffalo. Nobody in her high school would have voted her "Most Likely to Have a Buffalo Born in Her Front Yard." And if that buffalo happened to be white as a piano key and the only one of its kind in the world, well that was like icing an angel food cake.

But looking back, she could always see how even the most unexpected things work out in a way that makes sense, how the seeds of today's miracles were planted days or weeks or years ago. Maybe there's a big reason why the things we expect to happen five or ten years from now hardly ever come about, and why things we never would have guessed just work out naturally. Maybe that's why life is so interesting. The old buffalo hunters never would have thought the ocean they skimmed might one day go dry.

For example, Linnie grew up in the city without any pets. She stared, fascinated, when a dog brought its owner down to the streets for a walk. One reason she fell in love with Coy was the way any animal within a hundred yards—cats, dogs, horses, even a sharp-beaked cockatiel that fell out of the sky and landed on his shoulder—adopted him. He could charm a goat from a briar patch. The buffalo helped him train the horses even though some visitors thought he treated them like overgrown pets. And a casual act of generosity toward another buffalo owner resulted in Hope's birth.

So, looking back, the chain of events that led from her fascination with animals to Coy and his buffalo, made it seem almost inevitable that she would one day be midwife to a miracle.

But sometimes she figured magic was just part of the routine on the Double C Ranch. She saw it whenever Coy pasted his butt in the saddle on old Doc's Patience and dared a cow to try to get past him.

Doc's Patience was like one of those mythical creatures that has the head of one animal, the legs of another, the tail of another. How else could he act like a limbo dancer, an acrobat and a defensive lineman all in one sweeping pass? If not for magic how could a thousand-pound horse bob and rise like a champagne cork at sea? How could an animal that big find such speed and grace?

Kenny leaned against the fence next to Linnie and watched the magic game unfold every day, but the cow weaving in front of Doc's Patience had a different question. It wondered how could a horse be in two places at once?

"That cow's gonna wind up cross-eyed," said Kenny as he pressed his wrists against the fence rail over his head.

"Sh!" Linnie fluttered her hand at him. "Listen to the way he works her," she whispered. Linnie felt Kenny glance at her, but she refused to be distracted from the action in the arena.

Kenny had never thought about listening to a horse cut a cow before. After all, it was the sight of the athlete's bundled energy that made cutting so exciting. It was kind of like life: you never knew which way the cow was going to jump, but a top horse could find the answer to any move.

Now Kenny realized that the snort and sigh, the dull sound of the hoof sinking into the deep sand, and the bawling of the herd put music to the dance he loved to watch. He grinned and nodded at Linnie, but she was too absorbed in the scene to notice.

By the time Coy touched the horse's neck to signal that the game was over, the tips of his boots were dusty from scraping the arena dirt each time Doc swooped down to block a cow.

Doc's Patience was the horse that really launched Coy's career. The gelding was a little on the small side, but he was well-bred and soft-eyed. He'd been tangled up in a bitter divorce case that kept him out of training in the years when he might have been competing for the big money. By the time Coy heard about him, he was in a killer sale. Coy bid a few cents per pound more than the pet food buyers and took home a six-year-old that had scarcely been saddled since he turned three.

Coy put in a lot of time working with Doc's Patience, with little prospect of return. When the gelding began to fire, Coy hit the road to try to win the World Championship, a title given to a horse that might earn a hundred thousand dollars in a year in thousand-dollar chunks. Trouble was, the title quest blew most of his winnings on fuel, motels and truck stop breakfasts. Coy wore out his old pickup zig-zagging across the country to get to the next cutting.

Doc's Patience wound up the year ranked in the top ten. Coy didn't make as much money as he would have if he'd stayed home and given riding lessons to city kids, but no amount of money could have bought that rich, airy feeling in his chest when he rode Doc into the World Championship Finals with the best cutting horses on the planet.

One thing he'd never forget from that year was the way his radio would reel in the thin sound of the local country station as he drove into range of a new city. The coffee steamed the windshield when he set the cup on the dash and homed in on the signal. Thinking about the chicken fried steak at Lily's Cafe in Pocatello, Idaho still made his mouth water. And he'd always remember the feeling he got when he rode into that last arena on a horse that would make any man proud enough—and humble enough—to cry.

Now Coy had a shot at campaigning a horse the way it ought to be campaigned, starting at square one with the richest event in cutting, the Futurity. The Futurity purse added up to more than a million dollars, so it attracted the best of the best young horses. Stubby Hitchins could afford to buy any horse in the world with a price on its head, and when you got down to the nut crunching, that meant any horse in the world that Stubby wasn't feeding already. Stubby named the bay mare Money Honey and told Coy where to pick her up.

Coy would never tell another trainer this, but he liked to tie Money Honey where she could watch when Doc's Patience was working a cow. Coy knew as well as any man alive that horses learn by doing. Like people, they have to be a part of any lesson that's really going to stick. But, heck, there was something about this mare. She was special, and she was smart. Maybe it wouldn't hurt her to watch the way a seasoned pro like Doc worked a cow.

And maybe Coy would see if she didn't have some imagination, too.

Chapter 6
Courier of Good News

On an autumn day in 1953, B.K. Hitchins Sr. cursed and moved his foot to the brake pedal when he heard the siren behind him. Stubby felt a knot in his stomach as his father pulled over and held the steering wheel tightly in both hands at arms' length. The elder Hitchins looked straight ahead and breathed very, very deeply and deliberately as the trooper came to the window.

Stubby had never seen his daddy butt heads with any authority greater than his own. Stubby had never even imagined an authority greater than his daddy, and he didn't know what to expect.

"Can I see your license, sir?" The trooper touched the brim of his hat as B.K. fished his wallet out of his hip pocket. The officer disappeared for a few minutes while B.K. snaked a finger under his shirt collar and fumed.

"We've got some nice scenery in these parts if you take the time to notice it," the trooper said, startling both Hitchins senior and junior with his sudden reappearance by the car.

"It's even nicer on either side of these parts," B.K. said. "I have noticed that."

"I'm going to have to give you a ticket for speeding, sir."

"What's that going to cost me?"

"The court will tell you that."

"What? You don't know? Haven't you ever given a ticket before?"

"It'll cost you thirty-five dollars, sir, payable to the court."

"Then just write that ticket for seventy dollars and don't bother to stop me when I come through here tomorrow on my way home."

B.K. never had to lose his rough edges because he had money and the appearance of influence, which was usually as good as the real thing.

Stubby sometimes heard his daddy brag that his papers never backed a political candidate who lost. While the boast was calculated to leave the impression that B.K. was a king maker, Stubby discovered what he really meant years later when he was being groomed to succeed his daddy. In truth, the papers never stuck their necks out for unpopular candidates. Obviously, the winner of the election would have more backers, so B.K. could sell more papers by pandering to them. In close races, the editorial writers stressed the qualities of both candidates without ever climbing down from the fence.

Stubby adapted his father's dollar-sign diplomacy for his own purposes. Make everybody happy, was his motto, but make happiest those who could give you the greatest return on your investment.

For his part, Stubby was lucky to have business sense, because his sense of humor fell flat as the road to Lubbock. Built like a human cannon ball, with "STUBBY" tooled disarmingly into the back of his broad leather belt, he looked like he'd know all about fun. But he was so absorbed in details overlooked by the rest of the world that his punch lines couldn't draw blood from a hemophiliac.

His daddy bundled him off to an Ivy League school for a few semesters, but it didn't do much good. The yankees baited him so they could listen to his drawl. His fellow Texans fell into two camps. One group came from new-money families who hoped a little tradition and dignity would rub off on their best and brightest. The other camp came from old-money families who wanted to temper the wilder instincts of their prodigal children.

Poor Stubby couldn't have picked up tradition and dignity with a shovel. And he dozed off when the sons and daughters of established wealth began comparing the birth dates of their family fortunes, as if money were like wine that improved with age.

Turned out to be easier and cheaper to have Stubby tutored in the things he really needed to know back in Texas. They could teach him a lot of things, but not how to tell a joke.

"What the hell do you need a degree for anyway?" B.K. Sr. crushed his cold cigar in the ashtray. "Get yourself three hundred sixty of them and you're right back where you started."

B.K. Sr. took his brusque manner all the way to the grave. One posthumous cartoon which circulated in his papers' editorial meetings never enjoyed publication. It showed St. Peter looking glumly at the dime in his hand as B.K. strutted through the pearly gates.

Stubby never showed much interest in publishing, so when he inherited the empire he moved into other areas rather than expand his base of newspapers. For sentimental reasons, he couldn't bring himself to sell the papers. But to make it easier to remember which ones he owned, he renamed them all "The

Courier" one day not long after his daddy's death.

"Wouldn't it be great if the world only had one kind of news, and that was good news?" Stubby asked anyone who would listen, which meant everyone on his payroll. "I can't do too much about that, but I can make one kind of newspaper, and that's The Courier."

Stubby smiled, but the vice president, secretary or cafeteria lady who listened patiently to this, looked at him with a tentative, encouraging grin that turned a little sour when it became obvious that that was all he had to say on the matter.

Giving all of his papers the same name wreaked havoc in the editorial, production and legal departments, but it did have some advantages. For instance, the name Howard E. Gray meant nothing to Stubby, and one thing the tutors didn't have to teach him was that a rich man should never answer an unexpected call. But when his secretary told him that a Mr. Howard E. Gray was on the phone with an important message from the Coyoteland Courier, Stubby knew it was one of his own.

So he took the call that would change his life.

Chapter 7
The Eagle in the Iron

Although the grass really was greener in the front yard, Linnie finally coaxed Wanda to go back through the trampled section of the fence into the pasture. Hope skipped alongside her on spindly legs, looking more like a lamb than a baby bison.

"I tried everything on earth to get that buffalo to move." Linnie was still half exasperated by the time she and Coy sat down for supper.

"Did you try praying?" Coy propped his elbows on the table and broke apart a roll. "That used to work pretty good for the Indians."

"I tried alfalfa." Linnie rubbed the bridge of her nose. "That's what got her moving."

"Should have tried a buffalo stone."

Linnie dragged her hand away from her face. "What do you mean? Throw rocks at her?"

"Naw. A buffalo stone. It's some kind of magic deal. That's what it takes, you know, some kind of magic. If you fool around with buffalo much, it doesn't take long to figure out that they do whatever they want, and that doesn't necessarily have anything to do with what you want. Buffalo say you need help." Coy thumped his chest. "Buffalo say you not as smart as you think. Buffalo go to distant buffalo wallow in the full moon. That's when buffalo roll on ground and laugh at way man try to make buffalo behave."

"Did anyone ever tell you you're terrible?" Linnie shook her head slowly.

"No."

"Liar!" She narrowed her eyes. "I did. Many times. How do you know so much about buffalo?"

"You pick things up." Coy shrugged. "You make things up." Coy's eyes lit up. "I forgot—Thomas is coming by tomorrow to shoe the horses. He goes back to Chief Quanah Parker. I reckon he knows some things about white buffalo."

Thomas Eagle knew about a lot of things. He knew how to trim a hoof to make a lame horse walk. He knew how to find a lost cow in a thousand acres of scrub. He knew how to carve a guitar pick out of buffalo horn. He could scratch a wild dog behind the ears so that it would be in debt to him for the rest of its life. Coy had often seen a circle of kids close in on Thomas to listen to his people's stories about how the world came to be the way it was.

Thomas tucked a turkey feather in his hat and wore a beaded watch band. Most of his hundred-ninety pounds loomed above his diaphragm. Linnie always marveled that his arms were as big around as her legs. He looked like he could lift a horse and set it on the fence post to get a better shot at its feet.

Although Thomas' ancestors raced across the plains on unshod ponies, he felt at an early age that he had a mission to be a farrier. It took an artist to shape a glowing bar of metal into something that helped nature's most beautiful mover, the horse, fulfill its role in creation.

As his calling card, Thomas forged the outline of an eagle in flight into the bottom of each of his custom-made shoes. Coy was damned if the horses didn't look and act a little bit different after a visit from Thomas. They held their heads at a new angle and paid more attention to what people were trying to do with them. Their eyes brightened. Maybe it was just because the new shoes had fixed some lingering pain or imbalance. Then again, maybe it was something else. Coy had never seen results like that from any other farrier.

Thomas Eagle's business took him to hundreds of ranches in Coyote County and the surrounding area. His clients depended on him for news as much as for his blacksmith's skills. He knew everything that was happening in a hundred-mile radius and he could tell you faster than the U.S. mail and more reliably than the Coyoteland Courier.

Coy knew that Thomas had pulled into the Double C Ranch's drive even before he could see the pickup. The Double C dogs pricked their ears and sprinted for the gate. They escorted him enthusiastically to the horse barn, dashing and yapping just outside of the wake of dust the truck kicked up.

Coy and Kenny were watching Thomas nail the last shoe on Doc's Patience when Linnie hurried into the barn.

"Did you ask him yet?" she called. "Hello, Thomas."

"I was about to." Coy pulled his hands out of his hip pockets. "We've been busy fixing up these horses."

"Ask me what?" Thomas put the horse's foot down and straightened himself as Coy and Linnie exchanged glances. Kenny leaned against the stall and stroked the neck of the gray mare which had been watching Thomas work.

"We were wondering about buffalo—" Coy started.

"You've got more buffalo here than anyone I know," Thomas said, dusting his hands against each other. "I probably ought to be asking you about them."

"White buffalo—" Linnie jumped in.

Thomas narrowed his eyes at his clients to see if they knew some joke he hadn't heard yet. "Nobody's seen a white buffalo for years and years," he said at last. "Back when there were fifty million buffalo, there were a few, but they were always very rare. The white buffalo brought big magic. Isn't that right, Kenny?"

Kenny looked up as if the teacher had caught him napping in class. "I don't know anything about that Indian stuff," he said. "I'm a Texan."

"If you don't remember it, who will?" Thomas had a way of being very serious without being threatening. "Older people, their memory's not so good. The young ones are the ones who have to remember things, or else nobody will.

"You remember that spring a couple years back when the river cut off that mess of cows? Everybody told you to stay put, that the water was running too fast, but you rode old Lightning over there and led those cows back across the water."

Kenny shook his head. "That was nothing special."

"You were a damn fool, but you probably saved their lives." Thomas looked at Kenny steadily. "That's the first story Coy always tells folks if they ask if he needs some help out here. He says, 'Thanks, but I've got Kenny.' I've heard him say it a hundred times, but you probably haven't heard it once until now."

Coy kicked the dirt around in front of him, but nobody paid any attention to him as Thomas went on, "You did something bigger than yourself. Something any man who stopped and thought about it for a minute or two would say, 'I think I'll pass up on that offer.' See, that story is bigger than you are. Every cowboy in the world needs to hear a story like that because some day he's going to have to do something that would scare him clear into Oklahoma, and that story tells him that maybe he can swallow hard and do whatever it is that he has to do."

"Aw, but—"

"Sh!" Thomas straightened a finger in front of his mouth. "Being a hero doesn't give you a license to be rude.

"Now it's the same with our people. How did a man feel when he knew his children would starve unless he rode bareback at full speed through a herd of angry buffalo? A man couldn't see the ground for all the dust when the buffalo were running. One false move would toss him under the hooves. How many chances to die did that give a man?

"We don't know the names of those hunters, Kenny. But if we forget what they did, if we don't remember their lessons, then we'll lose something very important, something that we may find we need again some day."

Kenny listened carefully to all this and felt he was being persuaded rather than scolded. That was the way Thomas' magic worked.

But before Kenny could say anything, Thomas turned back to Coy and Linnie. "So, what's this about a white buffalo?"

"We've got something to show you," Linnie said, leading the men out of the barn.

"Sometimes buffalo would wallow in alkali pits so that if you saw them from a little distance—which was the safest way to see a buffalo anyway—they would look white," Thomas told them as they walked. "But the true white buffalo was sacred to most tribes."

"So the hunters wouldn't kill a white buffalo?" Kenny asked, taking three quick steps to catch up with Thomas.

"No. It's not like a sacred cow in India or anything like that. The sun and the buffalo gave man life, and each thing renewed itself. The sun left man at night, but always came back, restored. It was the same way with the buffalo. In its death, it sustained the tribe, but it always came back for another day.

"The white buffalo brought the hunter good medicine. It was a special gift to the hunter."

"Well don't tell any hunters about this," Linnie said, pointing to Wanda who rested alone like a small mountain in the open field.

"Did she have her calf already?" Thomas asked.

Wanda turned her head towards her visitors and then stood up so they could see Hope like a jewel glinting in the sun behind her.

"You can say that again," Linnie said.

Chapter 8
Staying Horseback

Linnie always said that Coy could outsleep a log, so it was unusual that he was the one who woke up that night. One second he was dreaming, and the next second he was staring at the ceiling.

The dream wasn't pleasant, but he couldn't call it a nightmare or anything like that. He found himself working on one of the big ranches back in the '50s, the way Cactus Gordon had told him things used to be.

"A man made sure he took good care of his horse back in those days," Cactus said when Coy was just starting out. "Nowadays some folks who call themselves hands will just go out and buy themselves another horse if the horse they're riding comes up lame or weak. Back then, they put you on the fencing gang until your horse could work.

"I tell you what, you've never had a vision of hell on earth until you've been out there trying to fence West Texas. That teaches you how important your horse is."

Coy nodded as he smoothed out a little tangle in Doc's mane. Then Cactus went on, "Course a ranch hand's horse isn't worth a nickel without cows, so you've got to take good care of them, too. Keep them strong and healthy. And a cow's not worth a nickel without good pasture, so you've got to watch your grass and your water.

"Fact is," Cactus said, tipping back his hat, "you've just got to make sure the whole world's working the way Mother Nature intended, or you're going to wind up afoot with a million miles of fences to cinch up."

These days a man could hang out his shingle as a cutting horse trainer even if he'd never laid eyes on a real working ranch. But Coy felt like the old ways, the ways that Cactus still believed in, gave you the foundation you needed to be a real trainer. How could you convince a horse to do what you wanted if you didn't take the time to understand what it wanted?

In his dream, Coy ran his hand down Doc's leg and felt the heat in the gelding's knee. He led Doc down to the creek and dammed up the water enough that it swirled up over the hot spot and washed the pain away. If this didn't work, Coy thought, he'd be walking the fences for weeks . . .

That's when Coy's eyes flipped open. He turned his head toward Linnie to see if she'd said something, but she was sound asleep. Coy felt thirsty. He sat on the side of the bed and thought maybe that was why he'd dreamt of water.

Coy liked the winter and spring because water still ran cold from the tap. In the summer the water came out hot; but then in the summer it seemed like he stayed thirsty enough that he didn't mind, as long as it was wet.

He drained the glass and set it back on the bathroom counter, but he nearly knocked it onto the floor when he turned out the light and saw the woman outside.

The Double C Ranch was miles from Buford, which wasn't much of a town in any case. You just didn't see many strangers wandering through your paddocks unannounced in the middle of the night.

When Coy got a grip on himself he leaned closer to the window and strained to see what was going on. The tall, striking woman stood near Wanda and Hope's paddock. Her long, black hair fell in a braid over the shoulder of her white jacket. If not for the jacket, Coy might not have noticed her in the moonlight. He watched, but she wasn't doing anything, just standing there.

Coy pulled on a bathrobe and boots. He looked at Linnie and thought about waking her, but then he thought that maybe he was still dreaming, in which case he didn't want to bother her. In the morning, he would find himself scratching his head as he tried to reconstruct that train of thought.

Coy slipped out the door and walked right up to the woman before she turned to face him.

"Ma'am?" he said. "Is there something I can do for you?"

The woman smiled and even in the sky's dim light, her teeth looked bright in contrast to her dark skin. "Thank you, no," she said. "Everything is okay."

"Um, I don't believe I know you, ma'am," Coy said, knitting his brow. "Are you lost or something?"

"Not anymore." She laughed. "I'm sorry. Please go back to bed. Everything's fine."

Coy looked at her for a long moment, thinking this must be the dream, and when he wakes up he'll be back in the creek trying to keep his horse from going lame. He lifted his arms a little bit and let them flop back to his sides. "Night, ma'am."

Linnie sighed when he climbed back into bed. She mumbled, "What is it, Coy?"

"Oh, there's a lady out in back," he said, staring at the ceiling.

"Here?" Linnie was beginning to wake up.

"It's okay." Coy touched Linnie's shoulder. "She said everything's okay."

Chapter 9
Fast News

In an information-starved world of high-speed communications, satellite relays and fiber optic phone lines, news can circle the globe in an instant. Fortunes that would have made the pharaohs blush have been spent so that Americans can tune in on events from the farthest reaches of the planet.

And in Coyote County, Texas, practically everybody knew everything before they saw it printed in the Coyoteland Courier.

If Howard E. Gray hadn't been an old geezer the day he was born, he would have been a young man when he took over the helm of the Courier, back in the days when it was still called the Coyoteland Gazette. He'd come into this world with a horrible congenital defect: he took himself seriously, even though nobody else did.

Except for two years when he went to Austin to study at the University of Texas, Gray had never spent a night outside of Coyote County.

"My roots run deep in Coyote County," he always wrote in his year-end State of the County message to his readers, "and they tap into a wellspring of printer's ink."

When he returned from Austin, he was hired as a copy boy and gopher by the newspaper's first editor, Hiram L. Cunningham whose snowy whiskers and green eyeshade framed a round, florid face. Cunningham gnawed at beef jerky around the clock and abandoned his typewriter only at meal times.

One morning, Cunningham squinted at a proof page and called out to his assistant. "Howard," he wheezed, "would you bring me a twenty-four point, upper case 'E,' please?"

Gray, who later learned to blame his chronic misunderstandings on a hearing problem rather than inattention, lugged a whole case of lead type over to his boss. Cunningham looked up perplexed and said, "Just an 'E,' Howard. I only needed one more letter."

Exasperated, Cunningham grabbed the type case from Gray and trundled across the office to put it away when the door opened on the unmistakable figure of B.K. Hitchins Sr. and a small boy. Cunningham's eyes swelled wide as moons as his breath turned ragged from the sudden exertion. "Just one more letter, Mr. Hitchins," he whispered before he keeled over, dropping the case on Howard's foot and spilling type across the floor.

B.K. ran next door to have someone summon a doctor, but it was way too late for that. After a flurry of excitement, Cunningham was carried out, and B.K. found Gray kneeling in the corner retrieving the scattered type. Gray plucked one letter at a time off the floor and studied it carefully as if trying to discern a message in the scrambled metal alphabet. He painstakingly replaced each character in its proper slot in the type case.

B.K. watched him a moment and said, "You know anything about running a paper, sonny?"

"Yes, sir!" Gray said, picking himself up from the floor. But just as he reached his full height, he tumbled over again. The case had broken his foot when Cunningham dropped it, and Gray was so eager to impress his new boss that he refused medical treatment for days. The incident left him with a limp for the rest of his life.

"You know how to spell and all that?" B.K. squinted at him.

"There's no better speller available in Coyote County." Gray admired the sound of his words.

"Know your way around town pretty good?"

Gray looked out the window at Main Street which was nearly as wide as it was long. "My roots are right here in Coyote County, sir!"

"I guess you're the new editor of the Coyoteland Gazette," B.K. said, extending his hand.

Folks who cared about news from outside the county's rectangular border could subscribe to a metropolitan daily, listen to the radio or watch television. Anyone curious about what was going on closer to home, could call Vivian down at the courthouse, come to town for a hair cut, or have Thomas Eagle drive over to shoe a horse. But someone who wanted to read the pompous, repetitive musings of Howard E. Gray on the subject of parking meters, or the changing seasons, or the dull performance of the U.S. Postal Service, had only to open the latest issue of the Coyoteland Courier.

Now things didn't really happen quickly enough in Coyote County to fill up a paper that came out every Tuesday and Saturday. One time, Howard E. Gray even committed to print the proposition that he and his media colleagues were steadfast in their use of their middle initials because that at least satisfied a tiny bit of the space that cried out to be filled before the next deadline.

So Gray always had an ear out for hard news, something he could put in his paper that wouldn't be a hand-me-down from the wire service. If he could just get on top of some breaking news, folks might stop snickering about his editorials. He might not get any more phone calls from anonymous teenagers on Saturday nights about UFOs and mutilated cows.

Gray had been with the paper twenty years when he had to grow a beard. He'd started balding prematurely, but he relied on his weekly trips to the barber to keep abreast of the local news he embellished and immortalized in the next edition of the Courier. His head still had white sidewalls, but he figured that having whiskers to trim would be good insurance against going totally bald and thereby losing his main source of information.

He was thumbing through Field and Stream and waiting for his turn in Bob the barber's chair when Olin Johnson asked what he thought about that white buffalo that was born out at the Double C Ranch.

"That's really something," Gray said, staring thoughtfully at the wall. After a moment, he closed the magazine and rubbed his chin with the back of his hand. "You know," he told Olin, "I've got a few pressing engagements this afternoon. Maybe I can make it until tomorrow without a trim."

Chapter 10
The Wail of the White Calf

Buffalo filled the plains in Kenny's dream. The great herd stretched out as far as he could see in every direction. Their musky odor clung to the dust churned up by their relentless hooves so that he had to tie his bandanna over his face to breathe.

The beasts trotted past him and Lightning at a pace that was calculated to see them through a long journey without exploiting their energy. He wanted to cry out, to ask where they were going, but he choked on the words, and he knew he could not be heard above the thunder of the hooves. The sound beat like a drum in the pit of his stomach so that his whole body became an ear to it.

The buffalo swarmed the landscape. He could see those close to him matching their exertion to the hummocks and slopes. Those farther away fit the earth like skin over rippling muscle. The brown tide split for trees and boulders and then flowed back into itself.

Atop one rock that broke the river of hides and horns, a white buffalo calf bleated. Her plaintive voice cut through the deep rumble of the stampede and struck a chord in Kenny's breast. The wail found a human voice that called to him in confusion. The calf did not know where the buffalo were going or whether it should join them. With its supple, white hide, the calf did not know if it even belonged to the same world as the dark, coarse-haired masses that lumbered past her. Was it beautiful, or some awful freak? Surrounded by a million cows, it felt abandoned by its mother.

Kenny felt terror of his own. The herd split to flow around him and Lightning, but the slightest movement would pull him under the churning hooves to certain death. The ground lurched and rolled beneath him. He closed his eyes, but felt dizzy. When he opened them, he felt worse. The wail of the white calf pierced his heart and he felt helpless.

Lightning, who could stare down a rattlesnake, began to rear up and Kenny felt himself falling backward.

He woke up with a gasp. He felt his heart racing out of control. His eyes searched his dark bedroom, but for a moment, he was afraid even to move his head.

It was three in the morning, but he couldn't get back to sleep. He dragged himself into the kitchen and took a whiff of the cold pot of coffee that he'd been working on for two, three days. He grimaced and dumped the dregs down the drain, thinking, "This isn't right. I've got to change some things around here." But he wasn't sure himself what it was that needed changing.

Kenny had always figured that either Coy never slept or he was twins. Today was the first time Kenny ever got to the barn before his boss. Kenny took a moment to enjoy the sound of the horses eating. Sometimes he figured the deep resonance of their grinding teeth satisfied him as much as it did the horses.

He saddled Lightning and had half the day's cattle gathered before Coy finally came down from the house and did a double take. "You know, we don't pay any more on the night shift," Coy said.

"Couldn't sleep," Kenny said. "Seemed like a waste of time being in bed like that. The radio doesn't even play any decent music this early."

*

Mr. Hitchins had paid six figures for Money Honey, a mare that had the breeding and the look of a Futurity champion. Coy was also training a colt for Mr. Hitchins, plus a mare which Linnie had bred, and a palomino gelding for Thomas Eagle. Kenny had his own mare, Fresh Freckles, that he planned to take to Fort Worth. It was going to be Kenny's first try in the Futurity.

Coy figured Mr. Hitchins made a good owner. Mr. Hitchins knew that he didn't know anything about training horses, so he let Coy get on with the job however he saw fit. He rarely even came to the ranch to see the mare he'd invested a king's ransom in. And Mr. Hitchins was generous, too. He was paying the entry fees on all of the Double C three-year-olds except for Thomas Eagle's gelding.

Coy started warming up his older horse, Doc's Patience, and told Kenny to bring all the three-year-olds out of the barn.

"All of them?" Kenny frowned.

"Yeah."

Kenny led them out of their stalls one by one and tied them along the fence, muttering to the dirt the whole time. The lost sleep was coming back to haunt him now.

"Where's your mare?" Coy asked when Kenny had finally stopped and leaned against the fence to glare at the boss.

"Aw, she doesn't need to watch this."

31

"She's set to win the Futurity already, is she?"

Kenny punched at the fence post, but pulled his fist back just before his knuckles smashed into the metal. "I swear I don't know what you think these horses are going to learn from watching you. What you need is a cheering section."

Coy lifted his hat and wiped his sleeve along his forehead. "You sure do get grumpy when you miss a little sleep. Why don't you just humor me before I get tired of humoring you?"

Kenny squinted up at Coy for a good half minute, figuring how much he owed on his car, how much his remaining Futurity payments added up to, and whether the Lazy S still had that opening he'd heard about. He spat on the ground and went to fetch Freckles.

Coy always wanted the young horses to watch him cut a cow with Doc's Patience, as if they might learn something from that. Everyone in the world busted out laughing when Kenny told them about it. How did he ever get stuck working for a crackpot like this?

The three-year-olds were just finding out what cow sense is all about. Some horses will cut anything that moves. There were stories about horses that would block a chipmunk that tried to cross their paddock. Back in the twenties, cowboys took bets on a horse whose owner claimed he could maneuver a rooster into a gunny sack. But most young horses needed to get used to the idea of working a cow, anticipating and mirroring any move it might make. It took months and months of patient work to bring them up to competitive level. It took years for a horse to really master the game.

"There's no substitute for a wet saddle blanket," Coy always said.

Money Honey was one of the naturals, but Kenny sure couldn't see that she'd picked up any moves by watching Doc's Patience. When Coy dismounted, he said, "Let's break for lunch."

"I'm not hungry."

"Suit yourself." Coy went into the house while Kenny loped Freckles to warm her up for her turn on the cattle.

Kenny let his mind wander as he circled the pasture, so he didn't notice anything until he practically ran over the old man who was waving his arms like a crow that was too drunk to fly. Freckles put on the brakes before Kenny did, but the man leaned sideways and swung his arms in big circles. Somehow he managed not to tip over, but his Stetson fell on the ground. Kenny blinked as the sunlight glanced off the top of the man's head.

The man nearly fell over again as he bent down to pick up his hat, but once again he found his balance. He brushed some imaginary wrinkles out of his clothes and looked up at Kenny. "Coy Cooper?" he said.

Kenny didn't say anything. He wondered what it was about this ranch, or about himself, that attracted so many damn fools.

"Howard E. Gray's the name," the man said, reaching his hand up to Kenny and lurching forward so that once again he nearly fell. He grabbed the reins for balance and Freckles wheeled around in shock. "I'm the editor of the Coyoteland Courier. Can you confirm or deny the reports of a white buffalo being born recently here at the Double C Ranch?"

Kenny waved toward the pasture where Wanda and Hope were. Mr. Howard E. Gray touched the brim of his hat and limped through the soft dirt toward the buffalo. When the man tried to stoop down to pick something off the ground, Kenny thought he was going to topple over for good.

"What's this?" the old man asked, squinting and fumbling with the thing in his hand. He held it up for Kenny and flapped his left arm for balance to steady himself.

Kenny took the colorful object from him. It looked like some kind of beaded bracelet, some kind of Indian thing. They were always finding arrowheads and whatnot on the Double C, but that stuff had been waiting in the dust for years and years. Something like this was too delicate, its colors were too fresh, for it to have been here very long. Kenny shrugged and mumbled, "Thanks."

Mr. Howard E Gray swung the gate open and stumbled a hundred yards through the pasture, circling around Wanda to get a better look at the calf. Kenny watched him stoop and peer at Hope, then duckwalk a little closer. Wanda turned head on to face the old geezer.

"She'll kill you if you get too close," Kenny shouted, startling Mr. Gray so that he plopped backwards onto his butt. He picked himself up again and staggered back toward Kenny, picking cockleburrs out of his britches the whole way. Freckles backed up a step when the man came near.

"The baby appears to be genuine," Mr. Gray said, blotting his face with a handkerchief. "When was it born?"

"Sunday night," Kenny said. "Or I guess it would be Monday morning."

"Much obliged, Mr. Cooper." Mr. Gray looked around to see where he'd parked his car. "I'll still make my deadline if I hurry."

33

"Mr. Gray," Kenny called to the retreating figure.

"Yes?"

"Your hat's on backwards," called Kenny, feeling a vague sense of guilt. "I thought you might like to know.

Chapter 11
Spreading the Word

This is Stubby," Stubby spoke softly into the phone. "How are you today, Mr. Gray?"

Stubby knew that most people expected near-billionaires to be loud and abrupt, as if they marked off their day with an egg timer that dropped silver dollars instead of grains of sand. In fact, he employed entire armies of overpaid middle managers and accountants to be rude and worry about time. One of the greatest benefits of being filthy rich was that he could afford to be nice to people. And by speaking quietly, embracing the ridiculous nickname he'd dreaded since childhood, and pandering to their vanity, he disarmed strangers. They fell to his mercy in an instant.

On his end of the line, Mr. Howard E. Gray breathed on the phone, shuffling the notes he'd made to prepare for this call.

"Hello? Mr. Gray? Are you there?" Stubby knitted his brow.

At last he heard a clearing of the throat on the other end. "My name is Howard E. Gray," the voice said, still a little syrupy. "I'm the editor of your paper, the Coyoteland Courier out here in Coyote County . . ."

"Yes, Mr. Gray, I'm familiar with your work." Stubby knew when to stretch the truth.

". . . where the West Texas sunshine comes right down into your boots . . ."

Stubby nodded and studied his fingernails.

". . . and nobody's stranger . . . pardon me, nobody's a stranger."

"I'm glad you called." Stubby made an exception to his usual protocol by raising his voice a smidgen. Perhaps, he thought, this poor guy is a little hard of hearing. "How is the paper doing? Are you keeping on top of things?"

There was another long pause before Mr. Gray said, "Fine. We've got everything under control out here."

Stubby's eyes wandered to the ceiling. There were some very intricate filigrees up there that he hadn't paid much attention to before. "Any big news stories breaking out there in Coyote County today?"

"Why, yes, as a matter of fact there is one." Mr. Gray sounded like someone had guessed the number he had thought of between one and ten. "We had a white buffalo born right here in Coyote County this week."

"Now, Mr. Gray, I own a few buffalo in Coyote County myself, and I happen to know that buffalo are brown."

"Well, this one is white," Mr. Gray tried to filter the irritation out of his voice. "I've personally verified that fact, at some risk to my person. And that's what gives the story its news value."

"So this is like a two-headed lamb being born, or maybe an image of the Virgin Mary appearing on a gas station wall? Is that right, Mr. Gray?" Stubby was becoming interested.

"I'm sure you're aware that the bison is an American institution, Mr. Hitchins—-"

"Please, call me Stubby."

"Yes, of course—-"

"Mr. Gray, do you have any uranium mines out there in Coyote County? Any toxic waste dumps? Any unusual convoys of tanker trucks pass through lately? Any reports of mutilated livestock? Do some of the kids have a problem with drugs? Anything at all?"

"Mr. Hitchins, before I lost my train of thought, I was going to explain that our county is a perfectly normal, wholesome slice of America. That's your news value! An extraordinary event in an ordinary setting. If something as remarkable as a white buffalo can happen here, well, who knows?"

"Who indeed, Mr. Gray?" Stubby rocked back and swung his feet onto the edge of his Italian marble desk. He flipped through his appointment calendar. He had lunch dates every day for the next six months, but nothing else that required his personal attention. "What's our next step, Mr. Gray?"

"The story will be in tomorrow's edition of the Coyoteland Courier, so I think a worldwide news embargo until then would be appropriate. After that, I think we should alert the networks and the wire services, and let nature run its course. Obviously, since the Courier will be breaking the news, our circulation should skyrocket. The value of your holdings in Coyote County could double or triple overnight."

Stubby tore himself away from Chez Verne's menu. "Yes. Right. You don't need me to tell you that you've done an outstanding piece of work, Mr. Gray." He fished through his drawer for a pencil. "Now where exactly was this white buffalo born?"

"At the Double C Ranch, owned by one Mr. Coy Cooper and his wife, Linnie."

"The Double C? That's where my buffalo are, Mr. Gray."

Chapter 12
The Woman in White

Coy Cooper wasn't absolutely sure that he'd been awake when he went outside in his bathrobe the other night, until he saw the woman with the white jacket talking to Kenny on Wednesday.

"Morning, ma'am," he said, touching the brim of his hat as he rode up and dismounted.

Kenny introduced her as Nancy McDonald. He looked at Coy, who looked back at him expectantly. Then Kenny mumbled something about watering the horses and he excused himself.

"So, you're a friend of Kenny's," Coy said after a moment.

"I hope so," Nancy said. "He seems like a nice young man."

One West Texas tradition held over since the frontier days was that anyone who showed up at your place was a guest. That put Coy in an awkward spot here. He sure didn't want to offend a guest, but on the other hand, he was mighty curious about why she was hanging around the Double C. "I don't believe I've seen you around Coyote County before," he said at last. "Except for the other evening."

"That's when I came in," she said, still smiling. "I live in Fort Worth."

"That's a good little drive to get some place that doesn't look much different from any other place in these parts. Do you have kin out this way?"

"I will pretty soon!" She laughed until Coy started to blush. "I'm sorry, Mr. Cooper. I thought you knew what was going on here."

"Heck, you must have me confused with my wife or Kenny," Coy said, lifting his hat to smooth back his hair. "Only thing I know is I'm the last one to know anything."

"I'm here because of the white buffalo," she said. "My uncle and some other men will be here tomorrow to offer prayers. This is a very sacred thing, a very wonderful thing for our people."

Coy nodded. "Who are . . .?"

"Lakota." She thought a moment and added, "The white buffalo is special for all Native Americans, but I know our legends best. We've been waiting for this, expecting it. You might say it's like the way Christians have been expecting Jesus to return. It's been such a long, long time that many people have given up hope."

Coy cleared his throat and looked over toward Wanda and her baby. They seemed oblivious to what people thought about them.

Nancy went on to tell Coy the story of Wohpe, the White Buffalo Calf Woman, who first appeared to two young men who were scouting for game one spring when the buffalo had been gone a long time. One of the men felt lust at the sight of the beautiful holy woman. When he went to her, Wohpe and the scout were swallowed up in a thick cloud, and when the cloud parted, the woman stood alone over the man's bones and the worms which had devoured him.

Wohpe told the other young man to go home and prepare for her arrival there. The people built a large tipi as she had instructed, and they waited for her. When the White Buffalo Calf Woman came she gave the people a sacred pipe and taught them many things. The pipe's bowl symbolized the earth. Its wooden stem symbolized the trees and plants of the world. A carving of a buffalo calf on the bowl symbolized four-legged creatures, and the pipe's twelve spotted eagle feathers symbolized all creatures with wings.

The holy woman explained that the pipe connected those who prayed with it to all other life. Man's feet tied him to the world of food and flesh, and the smoke which rose from the pipe tied him to the world of the spirit.

Wohpe also gave the people a stone with seven circles, each one representing a sacred rite in which the pipe would be used. She taught the people the first of these rites and told them they would learn about the others at the proper time. When she left the tipi, she ran across the prairie and turned into a buffalo whose coat was transformed from brown to white to black. And just as miraculously, the great buffalo herds which had been gone so long returned.

"Whenever people are troubled or quarrel," Nancy said, "they must remember the sacred pipe and how it binds man to all living things, so that all life is in harmony. It teaches us what nature gives, and what we must do in return."

"And you think this white buffalo is this holy woman?" Coy asked, trying to get this straight. "That she's come back to you like this?"

Nancy shrugged and smiled. "It's a sign," she said. "The most important thing to learn is that we always have more to learn."

Now it was Coy's turn to laugh. "Smartest man I ever knew reminds me of that every time I see him," he said.

Chapter 13
Mending Fences

The dogs didn't bother to bark. They just sat in the shade of the live oak and watched the gray truck come up the drive to the house. Coy rode Doc's Patience over and dismounted as the two men rubbernecked in the pickup. "Fine Fencing Co." was hand painted on the truck's doors above a patch of mismatched color with a phone number.

"Franklin Fine," the driver tugged off his work gloves and extended his hand, "I'm the chief operating officer of Fine Fencing Company but I hope you'll call me 'Frank.' I'm here to personally supervise your fencing challenge. And this is my associate," he waved the other man around to meet Coy, "Orwell Fine, but you can call him 'Bubba,' can't he, Bubba?"

Bubba nodded and held out his hand for Coy to shake.

Frank was a burly, slow-moving man who clasped his hands behind his back and planted his legs wide apart, as if he were trying to look a little shorter than his actual height. Although the day was sunny, with the promise of a hot summer to come, Frank wore a black felt hat and an insulated vest. The dust and sweat that coated his jeans and boots spoke of a workingman's life, but months later Coy would reflect that he never actually saw Frank do any physical labor.

In contrast, Bubba wore a Fine Fencing Company gimme cap and a western shirt fresh from the ironing board. His starched denim jeans were tucked into ostrich skin boots that had seen more honky-tonks than fencing gangs.

"We figured it out one time," Frank was saying, "And between us, we've fenced more of Coyote County than any two men alive. You know Dub Carson, down twenty mile south of here?"

"I don't believe I do," Coy said.

"And here, I thought everyone in the world with a horse knew old Dub," Frank said, screwing up his face in disbelief. "Well, we did his whole place for him. Those fire ants had gotten into his posts and eaten away at them. It was just a real mess. We had to tear out every rotten post there was, then we fenced it and cross-fenced it to where most folks consider it a real fencing showcase today."

"Like I said on the phone, we just need a little repair work done on a section of the cyclone fence over by the house," Coy said. "Had a buffalo come through it the other day when she was having a baby."

"Oh, Mr. Cooper! You can't keep a buffalo out with a little cyclone fence." Frank shook his head. "They'll be plowing through there like New York City cab drivers. You'll have us out there mending that fence every time you turn around. What you really need is our top-of-the-line buffalo fence."

Coy squinted at him. "Buffalo fence?"

"That's right." Frank started pacing next to the truck like a man without knee joints. "It'll stand up to an elephant, but you don't see any elephants in these parts, so we just call it buffalo fence. It's the only way to keep them critters where you want them."

"I believe we'll take our chances on just patching up the cyclone fence," Coy said. "We've had Wanda going on seven years and this is the first time she's tried to come up by the house. We've had twenty head of other buffalo here for three, four years, and never even seen them from the porch."

"Whatever you say, Mr. Cooper. We always say we believe in doing right by our customers," said Frank as Bubba's gaze wandered back to Coy.

Frank pulled his work gloves on as Coy led the men around to show them the damage. Linnie came onto the porch and watched to make sure Coy had them do the job right. He was such a pushover.

Frank stared for a long moment at Wanda chewing her cud behind Hope. He clicked his tongue, took off his hat and held it over his heart. "Oh, I'm so sorry to see such a pitiful sight, Mr. Cooper."

Coy stepped behind Frank and looked over his shoulder. "What sight is that?"

"Why that poor little buffalo cull." He shook his head slowly. "Kind of makes you wonder what the Lord's thinking when he does something as cruel as that."

"What do you mean?" Linnie asked, surprising all three men who hadn't heard her come up behind them.

"How do you do ma'am? I'm Franklin Fine, the chief operating officer of the Fine Fence Company, but you can call me 'Frank.'" He began tugging off his gloves again.

"You can call me 'Mrs. Cooper,'" Linnie said impatiently. "What did you mean about the Lord being cruel?"

"Well, those white buffalo haven't got very strong genes. They're just like a sickly child that wastes away and dies before it ever has a chance to live. That's why you never see any of them. The poor things don't live but a few days. Bubba and I have seen it happen plenty of times."

Bubba nodded. Then he swiped the cap from his head and held it over his heart.

Frank went on, "It's even worse if one of them white buffalo does survive because the rest of the herd won't accept it. They'll think it's some kind of wolf or something. Who knows what goes on in a buffalo's mind? Anyway, they'll fall all over each other to be the first one to stomp it to death. It's a horrible, horrible thing to see."

Bubba winced and looked at the ground as if the awful scene were about to unfold at that moment.

Frank shook his head sadly. "We could help you do the right thing here, Mr. Cooper. We know a place that would take care of that little cull in a humane way. All they charge is a small handling fee."

Coy glanced at Linnie, whose eyes were rolling like dice at Las Vegas. "I think we'll just keep her here," he said.

Frank cleared his throat. "I sure hate to see that, Mr. Cooper. I guess I'd be willing to pay that handling fee right out of my own pocket so that poor creature won't have to suffer anymore."

"So you guys are here to fix the fence?" Linnie said. "This part that's down on the ground is what needs fixing. The rest of it's fine."

Chapter 14
Buffalo Dreams

The dream haunted Kenny. It left him every night in sweat-soaked sheets with the pillow balled up next to his stomach.

The vast, relentless herd of buffalo swallowed up Kenny and Lightning. The white calf wobbled on its spindly legs on top of a boulder. It cried to him for help, but there was no way to reach it, and he didn't know what he would do if he could get there.

He became restless and irritable during the day. He stopped eating. He couldn't even find peace in loping Fresh Freckles. Kenny had never noticed it before, but Freckles was a little goose-rumped and ewe-necked. How was she ever going to win the Futurity built like that?

Coy scowled at him every morning and the horses picked up on Kenny's mood and mistrusted him. They baby-stepped to the back of their stalls whenever he walked in the barn.

Kenny felt silly, but he called Thomas Eagle about the dreams. At least silly was better than miserable.

Thomas stopped at the Double C between clients. He listened carefully to Kenny's description of the dream and how it made him feel. "Maybe you need a DreamCatcher," Thomas said at last.

Kenny thought that sounded like a member of an all-star baseball team or something, and that didn't make any sense. "Who is a DreamCatcher?" he asked.

"A DreamCatcher looks like a spider web," Thomas said. He explained how to make one by bending wood to make a hoop and then interlacing strips of sinew and beads to form the web. "You put it over your bed and it catches the bad dreams when they come to you at night. In the morning, the first rays of the sun destroy the bad dreams that are caught in the web. But good dreams can still travel along the spiral path to find you."

The trouble with Thomas was he never smiled so you could never tell when he was laughing at you. Kenny was starting to wonder if feeling silly really was better than feeling miserable.

"You know what, Thomas?"

"What?"

"That's about the craziest thing I ever heard of."

"As crazy as a young man who lets a dream steal his strength and happiness? How crazy is that, Kenny? Dreams should give you energy, not suck it out of you."

"What do you know about it anyway?" Kenny snapped. "You've never had a dream like this. It's so real I feel like I'm going to die."

"Even bad dreams don't want to kill you. They want you to understand them."

Kenny took his hat off and swung it as if he were about to throw it on the ground and crush it under his boots, but he stopped himself and put it back on his head. It was the best hat he ever had.

"That's why I called you in the first place, man," frustration edging his voice, "because I don't understand what in the hell is going on."

Not only did Thomas never smile, he never blinked, either. "What do you see in your dream?"

"I told you."

"You told me what happens, but what do you see? What's the dream trying to tell you?"

"I give up!" Kenny threw his hands in the air. He kicked the dirt and turned to go back to the barn.

"What are you afraid of?"

Kenny looked over his shoulder. "I'm afraid someone will see me talking to you and they'll lock us both up."

"Don't you feel the same fear as the white buffalo in your dream?" Thomas asked.

Kenny turned around slowly. "I guess I do. What's wrong with that?"

"Nothing's wrong, Kenny. Maybe you are the white buffalo? It's different from all the others, but it's the same in many ways, too. It doesn't know if it should join the herd and lose itself in the stampede, or if it should stay apart and hold on to those things that make it special."

"I still don't get it. What's that got to do with me?"

"Maybe the dream is asking you to decide who you are, Kenny. It's asking if you're going to abandon the Indian part inside you."

"I don't have an Indian part inside me. I got straight, black hair from my

45

grandma, and that's it. I can't even remember what tribe she's from. I've never been near a reservation. I went to school in town and dated a red headed cheerleader. I don't know which end of a bow and arrow is which. I'm just a Texas cowboy and that stuff has got nothing to do with me."

"Then why won't it let you sleep at night?"

Chapter 15
Coyote Town

Stubby could have afforded to start off big, but he took his first stab at building an empire in West Texas. The area was so sparsely populated that he figured he could experiment a little and make a few mistakes without attracting much attention.

The county seat was in Buford, over in the southeastern corner near Kent County. So Stubby staked out a tract of land in the geographic center of Coyote County and built Coyote Town from the ground up.

First a couple of signs which said, "Now Entering Coyote Town. Business District Ahead," rose up from the roadside scrub. Then the earth movers came, as loud and irresistible as a buffalo stampede. Arrowheads rose to the surface like flowers that had been sown a lifetime ago.

A patch of West Texas that hadn't changed in decades suddenly had a glittering truckers' oasis, a steak house, livestock auction barn, gift shop, movie theatre, petting zoo, and an office complex which housed real estate, accounting, insurance and law firms. Stubby scooped a hole in the plains, filled it with gyp water and built a marina. He built housing tracts with winding streets aimed at families in three distinct income levels. Coyote Town's brochures bragged of clean, modern schools, one of the nation's finest rural medical clinics, and the state's lowest local sales tax rate.

Coyote Town could boast that it had no crime, unemployment or social problems. Unfortunately, it didn't have any people either. Nobody really had much incentive to pull up roots and settle in the middle of nowhere, no matter how nice the facilities were.

That didn't faze Stubby one bit. For him, Coyote Town was an oversized architect's model, with the advantage that you could actually walk around it and enjoy the look and feel of an experimental city from a human's perspective. In one way, Coyote Town grew out of Stubby's fantasies that went back to the days when he played Monopoly while his daddy drove the Olds across West Texas. In another way, it was a logical blend of the old and new Texas: a pre-fab ghost town, a city that sprang up with neither a history nor a future.

Although the truck stop turned a profit, and the office complex held on to a few tenants, Coyote Town would have been nothing but a playground for rattlesnakes if not for Hollywood. Several times a year, one studio or another would lease the town as a movie set. It was especially popular for science fiction films in which dangerous experiments with germs or genes threatened to wipe out the human race, leaving only the trappings of civilization behind.

The studios also liked Coyote Town because their insurance rates were lower when the special effects crews worked with explosives. To the untrained eye, there wasn't much difference between West Texas before a ton of dynamite and West Texas after a ton of dynamite so they could blow things up over and over until they got it on film just the way they wanted it.

But for Stubby, Coyote Town was just a warm up. He bought entire city blocks in Houston, Dallas and Fort Worth, gutted the old buildings—or leveled them if necessary—and created something new. He talked about "life malls" where people worked and shopped and played without ever having to go outside if they didn't want to. His daddy, who had cursed those endless drives across West Texas, would have been proud.

Stubby owned an island in the gulf that showed up only on navigational charts. He built himself a luxury retreat where everything appeared to be as close as possible to its natural state. The roofs of the compound's buildings were even camouflaged so that they were practically invisible from the helicopter that shuttled him in and out. Stubby and the chopper pilot were the island's only visitors except for the occasional supply boat, and Stubby sometimes toyed with the idea of learning to fly himself.

He had vague ideas about Noah's Ark in mind when he began stocking the island with pairs of exotic animals, but he soon decided that was unnecessarily restrictive. A pair might be sufficient for giraffes, but when it came to gazelles, you needed to see at least fifteen or twenty springing across the prairie to really do them justice.

The island showed up simply as a parcel of undeveloped real estate in some master list of the assets of Hitchins Enterprises. That meant that every few years Stubby had the minor expense of finding some common ground with an auditor who asked too many questions. It was no big deal in the scheme of things, but to Stubby, it was a kingdom unto itself. Like the wildlife that would have fetched top dollar from big game hunters, Stubby could go there and drop his guard in complete safety. When you got right down to it, trying to make people like him was just plain hard work. He needed to get away once in awhile.

Contrary to popular opinion, being rich wasn't fun all the time. Making more money wouldn't cure Stubby's blues. Nor would taking more vacations because he didn't spend that much time on Hitchins Enterprises business anyway.

So Stubby spent most of his life on the look out for some other kind of compensation, something that he could give himself for his own happiness, just as he had tried to give others happiness. It didn't seem too much to ask, for one of the richest men in the richest nation in the world to own one thing that nobody else had.

Chapter 16
Wanda and Hope

// Those guys give me the creeps," Linnie said, folding her arms and shivering in spite of the spring warmth. "I don't know if I even want those guys working on the fence. I can't believe they'd come out here without a post wrench or whatever it was they said they had to go back for."

"Oh, they'll be okay with the fence," Coy said half-heartedly. "Some people just don't know much about buffalo."

Coy didn't have much of a handle on the subject himself when he got Wanda seven years earlier, but he'd been learning.

The buffalo was friendly. Cowboys on the great trail drives of the nineteenth century often reported that buffalo would tag along with the cattle for company, showing a herd instinct that crossed species lines.

The buffalo was curious. Some buffalo hunters were unnerved by the way their quarry might walk right up to investigate the butchering of their herd-mates.

The buffalo was cagey. Old timers said that several buffalo might charge a horseman, but if the rider called their bluff and charged back, they would veer off and run to safety.

The buffalo was challenging. The Pawnees told of the time their hunters spent months searching the usual hunting grounds for buffalo only to return home and find their villages overrun by the beasts.

The buffalo was hardy. It ranged from the mountains to the plains, from the snowy, windswept north to the broiling heat of Texas.

And for trainers like Coy, the buffalo made an ideal "cow" for a horse to practice cutting. Maybe it just enjoyed the game as much as the horse. In any event, it could be cut repeatedly without going sour like cattle. So the trainer could save a great deal of his livestock expenses by supplementing his herd with a few buffalo.

Coy cut his first buffalo when he was working for Cactus Gordon, the acknowledged master of the sport of cutting. Cactus had been phenomenally successful in competition, but his philosophy and his vast experience had made him a living legend. He applied principles he found in history and literature, politics and psychology to the sport of cutting. Young trainers flocked to him for advice. He had a waiting list of those who wanted to work for him.

"Remember you're supposed to be enjoying this," he always told them. "And don't be afraid to learn something new."

Training horses is a tough business. Coy was still struggling when he finally felt ready to set off on his own. One day, not long after he and Linnie had settled in at the Double C, Cactus came up the drive with a two-horse trailer.

"You might be needing this," Cactus said as he opened the door so that Wanda could back out. "She'll teach your horses a thing or two, even if you don't." Cactus winked at Linnie.

When Coy finally landed Stubby Hitchins as a client, he was able to forget about the economic constraints, but he still liked the way a buffalo tested a cow. Stubby bought a small herd from Bryan Bryson in Wyoming and put them at Coy's disposal.

Bryson raised a few buffalo back home, but he was known all over the country for a traveling show he put on with Byron the Bison. Byron's mother had been killed by poachers when the calf was just a few days old. Bryson raised him on a bottle and turned him into a pet. As Byron grew bigger, Bryson taught him a wide repertoire of tricks, from playing dead, to sitting on his haunches, to stamping out the answers to simple math problems.

The World's Smartest Buffalo became a local, then a regional and finally an international celebrity. Bryson took him on the road, giving exhibitions at shopping malls, sports events, festivals and fairs. The show included a sobering message about how close America had come to losing the buffalo forever.

"No nation in the history of the world owes so much to one animal as America owes to the buffalo," Bryan said as Byron nodded his enormous, shaggy head. "But by the end of the 1800s, after years of slaughter, there may have been only a few hundred buffalo left in North America."

At that, Byron always lowered himself to the ground and rolled onto his side, thrashing the air with his legs. His death act never failed to give the crowd goose flesh.

With a celebrity buffalo in his trailer, Bryson couldn't just pull into a motel at night as he criss-crossed the country between engagements. Stubby Hitchins had contracted him years before to put on an exhibition during Coyote Town's grand opening ceremonies. And Stubby later bought his herd from Bryson. So it was only natural that Bryson would make the Double C Ranch a regular stop over when his travels took him through Texas.

Bryson had grown up with buffalo, and he'd read everything about them he could get his hands on, but he'd never seen a horse cut one out of the herd until he met Coy. The books said that the thing that got the wandering buffalo of the old days most excited was water. It was no hardship for buffalo to go a day or two without a drink in cool weather, but they would charge for ten miles when they finally caught the scent of water after a long roam on the plains. It looked to Bryan like cutting tapped into some of that exuberance.

"I do believe that buffalo would pass up a drink to dance with your horse," he told Coy who rode Doc's Patience while Wanda lunged and feinted in the arena, trying every trick to get past him.

"I reckon this horse would go without grain to dance with that buffalo," Coy replied.

The sight of the two animals locked together in motion sowed the seeds of invention with Bryson. It was like a ballet from some fairy tale where humans were unnecessary, adding nothing to the natural grace of the beasts. There must be a way, he told himself, to work a cutting horse into his show.

Bryson stopped by with Byron the Bison several times a year, and each time he asked to see another demonstration of buffalo cutting. Coy was glad to oblige. In his idea of heaven, the angels wore chaps instead of wings, and you never cut a sour cow.

One day, months after Bryson's last visit, a courier arrived with an unexpected package. Coy was out in the pen, so Linnie signed for it. She asked the delivery man what it was, but he shrugged and said, "They're all the same to me."

Linnie didn't think Coy would want to be interrupted, so she set the package on the kitchen table, then spent forty-five minutes tidying the house. The chores seemed to keep bringing her back into the kitchen. When she realized she'd been over the kitchen table with a damp rag three times in the last nine minutes, she picked up the box and stormed out the door.

"Were you expecting a package?" she shouted.

"What?" Coy was studying some piece of leather or something.

"Were you expecting a package?"

"Oh. No."

"Will you get your butt over here and open this, Coy Cooper?" Her voice rose.

"Okay, okay." Coy rode over to the fence and said, "What is it?"

Linnie rolled her eyes. "It's addressed to you."

"Oh." He fumbled with the cardboard shell and peeked inside without learning much. He climbed off Doc's Patience and flipped open the metal box inside.

"What is it?" Linnie couldn't help acting like a kid on Christmas morning.

Coy held the note out at half an arm's length to focus on it. "Says here it's buffalo semen. Bryan says he thought we might like to try breeding our own buffalo."

"Oh," said Linnie, stuffing her hands in her pockets and looking over her shoulder.

And that's how Wanda was introduced to motherhood.

Chapter 17
The Hero Lightning

Like every other night—like every time he closed his eyes—Kenny found himself in the midst of the buffalo. The herd stretched for miles in every direction. Their hooves had turned the plains into powder as fine as talcum. They seemed to pass him in slow motion as if they would never end. But every time Lightning shifted his feet, Kenny's head spun as the thundering mob's true and deadly speed became apparent.

Through the choking brown haze that rose like a river fog around him, he caught sight of the white buffalo calf. Her thin, reedy voice cut through the deafening roar, as it always did. It called for help, as it always did. Kenny felt helpless, as he always did.

This time, with his bandanna pulled over his nose to filter out a little of the dust, it occurred to Kenny that if anyone else came to answer the cry of the white buffalo, he was in danger of being mistaken for a bank robber. The situation was so complicated, and he hadn't asked for any of it.

Kenny leaned forward and rubbed his cheek against Lightning's mane. He stroked the horse's neck. "What are we going to do now, partner?" he asked.

In a flash of relief and exhilaration that seemed to stretch on for days, Lightning arched his neck and whinnied. He pricked his ears and took in the hide-bound panorama before them. Kenny grabbed the saddle horn with one hand and waved his hat in the other. He cried out, "Ya-hooo!" as Lightning reared and leaped into the air.

Lightning landed on the hump of a charging buffalo bull. In an unbroken motion, he tucked his legs in and flew to the back of another buffalo a little closer to the white calf.

Lightning carried Kenny over the herd as if were landing on stepping stones to cross the rapids. The earth itself came alive beneath their feet and the whole universe swirled into motion around the calf. Kenny felt like he was running up the down escalator as each jump that Lightning took was nearly canceled by the onward charge of the buffalo he landed on before he could bound again. And yet, all of creation seemed to be conspiring to carry Kenny and Lightning to their goal. Leaping from one moving target to the next, Lightning's feet never missed their mark.

Even as they inched closer, the white calf's cries grew more desperate. Kenny feared only that the baby's spidery legs would betray it and it would fall beneath the blind, trampling hooves to certain death.

"Hold on, little buddy," he called out as Lightning whinnied. "Hold on!"

At last they came within range. Kenny leaned over sideways in his saddle as Lightning landed on the boulder. Lightning's steel shoes threw up a shower of sparks as they struck the stone. Kenny scooped the calf up effortlessly in one arm, feeling strong enough to lift a full-grown bull half way to the sky if the need arose.

In a broad, seamless motion, Lightning sprang from the boulder and carried Kenny and the calf to the back of the next buffalo. He leaped again and again, galloping tirelessly against the brown buffalo tide.

The calf snuggled against Kenny and licked the hand he held out to steady it.

It would be a long journey, but Kenny knew that Lightning would not give up until they'd regained solid ground.

Kenny woke before the radio came on with its old-time country music. His eyes sparkled even before he brewed a fresh pot of coffee. He felt refreshed and clear-headed, but the sight of the DreamCatcher suspended over his bed startled him. He'd forgotten that he'd put it there last night.

He stared at it for a moment, then smiled.

"Well, I'll be . . ." he said out loud.

Chapter 18
Fine Fencing

Frank and Bubba of the Fine Fencing Company became virtual commuters to the Double C Ranch. They kept forgetting this tool or that material they needed to fix the fence Wanda had trampled.

At first, Linnie made a point of glaring at them from the front porch, but they showed up so often and made so little progress that she couldn't spare the time to do that.

"You guys aren't much good at this, are you?" she said as she passed Frank in the afternoon.

The shock and wounded pride sent Frank's jaw halfway to his trophy belt buckle. He fiddled with his work gloves for a long moment, trying to get them to fit just right, before he could answer.

"I can't believe you would say such a thing, ma'am. We are proud members of a highly technical profession. Fencing technology is making some of the greatest leaps forward in the world today. Why, do you know what the difference is between a fencing technician and an engineer?"

"I'd guess about sixty IQ points."

Frank didn't seem to hear. "The difference is that an engineer can go to school and have someone spoon-feed him everything he needs to know," Frank said solemnly. "There's not a single school for fencing technicians in the entire United States of America. We have to do it all by ourselves. Heck, ma'am, did you know that your federal government flat refuses to give the fencing industry any tax relief whatsoever? Most people have no idea."

"No kidding." Linnie scowled, but Frank seemed to be blind as well as deaf.

"Not a nickel. And where would this country be without fences? You should ask your congressman if he ever wondered about that."

"I'll call him today," Linnie said, brushing past him in exasperation.

Frank nudged Bubba when Linnie was out of earshot. "You know you can help me out here once in awhile," he whispered.

Bubba shrugged and they ambled over to the fence which wasn't looking much healthier than it did the first time they visited. They spent a lot of time studying Wanda and the white calf in the field, making a pretense of looking busy only when Coy or Linnie or Kenny came into view.

When the coast was clear, they stepped gingerly into Wanda's pasture, freezing whenever she turned her head in their direction as if they thought she couldn't see them if they weren't moving. They approached her cautiously, lifting their knees high and easing their feet into the grass, wobbling their arms to keep their balance. Every now and then Frank brought a finger to his lips and shushed Bubba who hadn't uttered a word in two days.

As they moved within twenty yards, Wanda turned to face them and Hope peeked around her butt. Frank froze so quickly that Bubba jostled his shoulder. Frank turned to scold him, but before he could say anything, they heard Wanda's first snort of warning.

Wanda lowered her head and pawed the ground and Frank imagined he could see jets of steam blasting out of her nostrils. They hadn't worked out any particular escape plan, but Frank high-tailed it one way and Bubba another so that Wanda had only to lunge forward a few steps to disperse the danger to her calf. She circled back and snuffled Hope while the fencing technicians reunited at the pickup, slammed the doors behind them and spun great plumes of dust from their back wheels as they swerved back to the road.

Chapter 19
The Gift

Stubby believed in making his people happy. He firmly believed that was the most important part of his success in business, and yet he shared his "secret" freely with the press. It was something that most other tycoons, and especially the corporate takeover sharks, could never quite grasp. They wanted a chart that would show them that X dollars spent on employee happiness would result in a Y increase in productivity. Stubby's genius, his contribution which could have revolutionized capitalism, was that he didn't need any more money so he wasn't concerned whether smile-dollar expenditures were exceeded by widget-dollar receipts. All he knew was that it was much more pleasant to be surrounded by happy people than cranks.

In fact, the equation did help boost his assets, but that was a byproduct.

And if he could produce the greatest happiness in his people at negligible expense, well, so much the better. That's why he went to the small trouble of picking up Howard E. Gray in the limo on his way to the Double C Ranch.

Gray's face looked vaguely familiar to Stubby who couldn't imagine where he might have met the man before. For his part, Gray had also forgotten the first time they'd seen each other, that momentous day when Hiram L. Cunningham expired and control of the Coyoteland Gazette—now the Coyoteland Courier—passed on to Gray.

"Would you like an iced tea?" Stubby asked as the big, black car set off for the Double C. "Something stronger?"

Gray nodded his head, too awed to speak, too conscious of the syrup in his throat to even risk clearing his throat.

"Which?" Stubby asked. "The tea?"

He nodded.

"Sugar?"

He shook his head.

"Sweetener?"

He nodded.

"Twist of lemon?"

He nodded.

A veteran of discomfort in social settings himself, Stubby had a good handle on being gracious in difficult circumstances.

"We've been impressed by your work at the Courier for a long, long time, Mr. Gray," he stretched the truth as they leaned back in the plush leather upholstery. "Editors are about the hardest-working species in the world today. I've often wished I'd pursued the field myself. I've always admired men like yourself who can gather the news, present it objectively; who can shape public opinion with the sheer force of their persuasive powers," he went on, lying right to Mr. Gray's blushing face. He saluted Mr. Howard E. Gray with his glass of tea. "We have printer's ink in our veins. Medical science has found no cure for it, thank the Lord."

Mr. Gray nodded.

They rode across the West Texas miles and Stubby thought how different it was today than when he and his father had covered this same territory. Not the land—it hadn't changed in the slightest degree. But the chauffeured limo floated over the miles without noise or effort. The temperature and humidity were tuned in perfect harmony. The road seemed so impossibly smooth that Stubby imagined he could play Monopoly in the limo with a board that didn't rely on magnets to hold the pieces in place.

Coy was waiting for them by the barn when they pulled into the Double C. Stubby hopped out of the limo while the driver came around to give Mr. Gray an arm to steady himself.

"Coy, this is Mr. Howard E. Gray—" Stubby began. "But you've met already . . ."

Coy shook the stranger's hand as he and Mr. Gray puzzled at each other. In fact, Mr. Gray had mistaken Kenny for Coy when he visited the ranch to see the white buffalo before.

Coy led the visitors around to the arena where Money Honey was warmed up and ready to go. Without a word, he opened the gate, walked her straight to the herd. He drove a group of cattle away from the others and let them trickle back one at a time until the only one left was a bald-faced cow he'd picked out while studying the cattle before the company arrived.

Realizing it was alone, the cow tried to trot back to its companions, but Money Honey sprang in front of it. The cow, maybe thinking this was just a minor misunderstanding, a breach in animal etiquette, turned to go by in the direction the filly had just come from. Money Honey dropped her butt, swiveled and launched herself into the cow's path again. The cow jumped back the other way, but before it could cut across to the herd, Money Honey materialized in front of it again.

The two animals stood eyeball to eyeball. The cow hesitated, wondering how it was going to get past. Money Honey lowered her head and dared it to try. Her legs quivered in anticipation. She was like a hairpin trigger, ready to fire at the slightest command.

Stubby applauded while Howard E. Gray looked bewildered.

"She's already way down the trail for an April three-year-old, Mr. Hitchins," Coy said when the demonstration was over. "She's sure enough the best Futurity prospect I've ever had. Best one I've laid eyes on."

"Could you cut a few more for us, please?" Stubby asked, like a boy who gets a command performance at the circus. "I love this stuff. You just don't get much fun in town."

Coy was happy to oblige, but Mr. Gray grew impatient as his gimpy leg began to act up. "When is this going to end?" Mr. Gray whispered to Stubby while Money Honey drew an imaginary line and dared the next cow to cross it.

Stubby turned his head in Mr. Gray's direction before his eyes followed. "It never ends, sir," he said, quickly turning back to the action. "It never ends."

By the time Coy was ready to give Money Honey a break and take over on Doc's Patience, Mr. Gray couldn't stand it any more. He cleared his throat and said in a voice loud enough that whoever it concerned could answer, "What about the buffalo?"

"We use buffalo quite a bit," Coy said, missing the concern in his guest's voice. "But they're down by the creek just now. It would take awhile to gather some up to cut."

"The baby buffalo . . ." Mr. Gray lost his voice again.

"We've only got one baby on the place so far this spring, but she's way too young to cut." Coy rubbed his forehead and looked at Mr. Hitchins. "Fact is, I don't know if we'll ever cut with her. She's kind of different from the rest and I just haven't had time to think about what we're going to do with her."

Stubby didn't look at Mr. Gray, but he saw his opening. "How's she different?" he asked. "Is she okay?"

"Well, fact is, she's white as a cloud in July. I've never seen anything like it."

Coy tied his horse to the fence and led the visitors around to the field where Wanda grazed with her baby. He waved at the colorful gifts the Native Americans had left beside the fence for the white buffalo. There were feathers and ribbons, a carton of Lucky Strikes, jewelry, bundles of sage and sweetgrass, moccasins, smooth stones and incense, and all sorts of enigmatic objects made from beads, string, bark and wood.

"What's this?" Stubby wondered, pointing out a hoop with two cross bars and several dangling feathers.

"They call it a medicine wheel," Coy said. "The four branches of the cross represent the winds, the seasons, the four corners of the earth—I guess a lot of those important things come in fours. Those beads on the corners represent the races of man, black, yellow, red and white. Put the whole thing together and it's talking about harmony and balance, about the brotherhood of all people."

Stubby looked at Coy with wide eyes. Even Mr. Gray seemed impressed.

"I just found all this out the other day," Coy said, a little defensively. "A lot of folks have been coming through here to see this little buffalo." Coy gestured to the field and said, "Wife named her Hope."

"Isn't that something!" Stubby's enthusiasm almost roused Mr. Gray out of his funk. "Can we go over there?"

"Well, a little ways, but you'd best be careful. Buffalo don't mind a lot of things we do, but a buffalo mama is very particular about people messing with her calf. She's bigger than anything you'd want to have acting ornery around you."

The three men walked slowly within fifty yards of the animals before Coy waved them to a halt. Although there was no need to be quiet, Stubby whispered, "Is she one of mine?"

The question startled Coy, who looked first at Mr. Hitchins, then at Mr. Gray, and then back at Mr. Hitchins. "Why, no, sir," he said. "The mama was a gift from Mr. Cactus Gordon. The daddy was a gift from Mr. Bryan Bryson." He touched the rim of his hat. "And babies are always a gift from God."

Chapter 20
Cactus Lessons

"You might have a cow pony that can cut siamese twins back at the ranch," is the way folks often quoted Cactus Gordon, "but when you get to the Futurity, you have to know how to handle a crowd as much as a cow."

To initiate young horses to a scaled-down version of the sights, sounds and smells they will encounter at the Futurity, trainers often hauled them along with their older horses to local cutting horse shows. The older horses compete, the younger ones just get used to riding in the trailer, and to being on the perimeter of the action.

"It's like life, this cutting thing," Cactus told the young trainers who flocked to him, "the more of it you do, the more you can do. Same thing for your horse."

Cactus had quit school long before he started shaving. Since most able-bodied cowboys were in the service during World War II, a kid like Cactus could earn a Ph.D. in cow punching on any of the big ranches of West Texas. The old hands loved to show a kid how to flank a steer.

It was a perfect apprenticeship for Cactus. Even as a teenager, he sensed he was hanging onto the edge of something important that was about to slip away before the world knew what it had lost. The old hands couldn't tell you in so many words, but they knew how to keep in play the fragile balance of rain and grass, of stock and demand.

Cactus winced as the soothing clip-clop of a horse on the trail gave way over the years to the awful buzz of a two-stroke engine. The closest some so-called ranchers ever came to being bow-legged was when they held a cold, twelve-ounce can between their legs as they drove the pickup.

One time Cactus called the Coyoteland Courier to cancel his subscription. "What seems to be the problem?" the wavering voice on the phone asked him.

"This fancy, front-page story you did on Dub Carson yesterday says he has forty years of ranching experience," Cactus snorted.

"That's the information our editorial department received," the voice said. "But we live and die by accuracy in the publishing business. We'll print a retraction if you have proof that the statement is in error."

"Good! Because any fool who knows Dub Carson knows that he hasn't but one year of experience. It's just forty times over." Cactus was so mad he hung up the phone before he told the man where to stop sending the paper.

The only times Cactus got upset were when people started playing fast and loose with history, or the written record of current events. He'd left school at his first opportunity because the curriculum held him back. He soaked up the experiences of the last of the old-time cowboys while he made a living, and he read widely to put his life into perspective. He depended on the written word to be accurate and he had scant tolerance when it came up short.

By the time he signed on as a smooth-faced fifteen-year-old at the sprawling Flying U Ranch, Cactus was too late to meet anyone old enough to remember the buffalo days. Most of the men had driven cattle a little ways, but almost all of them were too young to have been on the great trail drives that defined America's image of its history and the West.

More than the world-wise cowboys who came back from the war, Cactus understood that their work held a significance beyond the daily routine. There was more to this life than just raising healthy cattle, moving them where they needed to be, taking care of the country, and collecting up a paycheck.

One August afternoon a few years after the war, Cactus was picking up strays with a man named Bo McClintock. McClintock was a pretty fair hand, but he always found something to grumble about. It didn't much matter whether the object of McClintock's ire was camp grub, low pay, long hours, the foreman, the rattlesnakes, or the stupidity of a cow that managed to get herself lost in the first place. In fact, McClintock's complaints came so frequently, that a man had to pay real close attention or he wouldn't be sure where one gripe ended and the next began.

"You're a might sour today, Bo," Cactus observed as they rode along behind some Herefords that would just as soon have been chewing their cuds as moving across the pasture.

"Better to be sour than a crazy damn fool is the way I see it." McClintock leaned to the side and relieved the pressure built up by his plug of tobacco. "A man'd have to be a crazy damn fool if he didn't hate chasing these pea-brained cows from here to kingdom come."

"Now, Bo, we're doing more than chasing cows out here." Even as a young man, Cactus couldn't keep the excitement out of his voice when he talked about his favorite subject. "We're preserving the American way of life right here on the

Flying U, just like you fellows were doing overseas a few years back."

"At least there we had someone to shoot at," McClintock groused. "Look at this!" He waved his arm through a half circle. "'Cept for you, there's not a soul within ten miles of this God-forsaken place. What are we doing out here with the sun bearing down on us, chasing through the prickliest dang mesquite on the face of the earth—all for some cows that nobody would ever miss if we just left them out here as rattlesnake bait, the way the good Lord intended."

"Thing is, Bo, we're here for more than those cows." Cactus smiled so wide that McClintock feared he might be going into heat stroke; and what a mess that would be. "We're here for kids in New York City who don't know a heifer from a horse. We're here for men that never tasted a cup of coffee an hour before sun up with their backs to the wind. We're here for all the people who live in town and wonder why, the ones who'd swap their souls for a saddle if they could see you out here in the fresh air all day doing whatever you dang well please."

"If I was doing whatever I dang well pleased, I'd be soaking in a tub in Buford with a bottle of beer in one hand and a big, old cigar in the other. What makes them city folk think we get to do what we want?"

"They're just hoping," Cactus said. "Maybe that's what we're here for, to give other folks some hope. Maybe if we weren't here, they'd hire us off the street and send us here, just so they could go to sleep at night thinking a man can still live a life where he's got choices to make.

"Soon as you ride over that horizon, nobody knows if you leave a calf to die because you're too lazy to get off your horse. Most people in this world don't get lucky enough to make life-and-death decisions, Bo."

The next morning, as McClintock rode out of camp with Herndon, Cactus overheard him saying, "You ever ride with Cactus? He'll get you out over that ridge and talk you to death before you ever have a chance to shout for help . . ."

Cactus learned a lot at the Flying U and the other big ranches. But one of his most important lessons was that most of the time, a horse learns a lot faster, and better, than a man.

Years later, when people came to him from the cities to learn how to cut a cow, he put them on an experienced horse and just watched enough to make sure they didn't fall off and bust their heads. The horse taught them a lot more than words ever could.

"It's like the horse is telling me to do this or that," the novice would say at the end of a lesson. "Maybe I should try blah blah blah—-"

All Cactus had to do was nod, collect his fee and buy enough hay and oats to keep his faculty happy.

And Cactus had always told Coy that a horse can teach a horse, too. A green horse might be flighty the first time it goes out in public. But the youngster will pick up the calmness of more seasoned horses around it. So Cactus, Coy and Kenny loaded up the trailers most weekends and took an entourage of Futurity prospects to the nearest cutting horse show.

At the time, there didn't seem to be any reason to make an exception for a baby buffalo.

Chapter 21
The Viewer

Once in awhile Linnie went to horse shows with Coy and the other guys, but usually she couldn't afford the time to go. The horses that were left behind needed tending, and getting Coy out of her hair for a day or two was the best way to keep the business afloat.

There are two kinds of horse trainer; and if not for Linnie, Coy would have fallen into the larger group, the penniless ones. Left to his own devices, Coy would bill clients once a year, if that often. Linnie suspected that Coy felt vaguely guilty charging for something that he loved doing so much. If not for Linnie, the feed shed would be empty, Thomas Eagle wouldn't be called until the horses had cast off all their shoes, the vet would need a map to find the Double C Ranch.

Usually a weekend with Coy on the road meant a little piece and quiet and a chance to catch up on things. But this time the truck and trailer had hardly turned onto the highway before things got busy.

It started with the helicopters. The first one flew low over the barn while Linnie was mucking out the stalls. The horses pranced and whinnied in alarm. Their ears twitched every which way as they tried to figure out what that god-awful noise was.

They didn't often have planes overhead, much less helicopters, but Linnie didn't think too much about it until she heard the chopper circle back a moment later and buzz past even closer to the ground.

She leaned the rake against the wall and hurried outside to see what was going on. While the first helicopter hovered over Wanda and Hope, a second one appeared from the west and began closing in on the ranch like a giant, hungry insect. Then it, too, went straight to Wanda's pasture. It dipped down to get below the first chopper, but that one sank, too.

The whirling blades churned up dust devils that circled around mother and baby. The buffalo began to trot for safety, but the two helicopters followed them, neither one giving an inch to the other. As Wanda did laps around the field, shaking her head to clear the dirt from her eyes, a third helicopter appeared from the south. The new one dogged the other two until Linnie feared they would all crash in a heap of twisted metal and shattered glass. She ran beneath them, waving her arms and shouting as if they were crows that could be chased away.

When Wanda and Hope reached a point not far from the house, one of the choppers broke formation and landed in the front yard. The pilot killed the engine and a woman in a smart-looking suit and a man with a camera climbed out, ducking their heads as they ran to Linnie.

Seeing this, the other two copters landed as well, and within moments Linnie found herself in the center of an impromptu press conference. Microphones spouted like mushrooms. Cameras zoomed in.

"What did you think when you saw the white buffalo—"

"—offers to buy—"

"—significance to Native American cultures—"

"—what are your plans—"

Linnie felt like the mother of hyperactive triplets. She didn't know where to look or what to say with everyone vying for her attention at once. She pressed her hands to her ears and screamed, "Shut up!" as loud as she could.

That worked.

The reporters grimaced. The camera men pulled back and inspected their equipment for sound damage or something.

"Everybody just be quiet. You're scaring the hell out of our livestock. Now will somebody please tell me what's going on?"

The reporters jostled closer and began blabbering all at once.

"You—" Linnie pointed to the woman who had emerged from the first helicopter. "Tell me what's going on here." She turned to the other two reporters and narrowed her eyes. "I break horses, you know," she said.

The men shuffled back a step.

"Okay," she said, turning back to the woman, "What is this?"

"Katie Kersinski, Channel Five Live—"

"You mean we're on the air now?" Linnie frowned.

Kersinski looked puzzled. "No, we're taping this for tonight's show."

"I get it. The show's live on tape. You have to go slow with me here. I'm just a country girl," Linnie lied. "So what is it you're trying to tape? A show on how to curdle buffalo milk?"

Kersinski fiddled with her left earring, a secret signal for her camera man to zoom in for a close-up of Linnie. "The white buffalo," she said. "This is extremely rare." She lowered her voice and edged closer to confide in Linnie, "We plan to use the footage from your ranch as a teaser for the ten o'clock news. Millions of viewers will see it."

"Well, Ms. Kersinski, you probably don't get around livestock too much, so you may be surprised to find out that we haven't heard the first word out of that little white buffalo, so I don't think she has anything very important to say to your viewers."

This was a tough call for Kersinski, who was infamous at the station for her quick wit and acid retorts. Her reflexes were itching for a put down, but she couldn't afford to alienate Linnie until she had what she needed. She fiddled with her right earring as a nervous gesture, but her voice held steady.

"Mrs. Cooper, sometimes people get swept up in great events. Things happen that have never happened before. That's why we call it 'news.' The world changes so fast that people are afraid they'll miss something and be left behind. My job is to help people keep up."

"Well, if people didn't know about this baby buffalo at all, then that wouldn't be news, would it?"

"This is something that's bigger than the Double C Ranch and Coyote County," Kersinski said, keeping her eyes wide and unblinking. "Besides," Kersinski waved at her fellow vultures, "you can't put the genie back in the bottle."

The other reporters knew Kersinski well. They inched forward, straining to hear.

Linnie signed in resignation. "In other words, you're not going to give us a minute's peace until you take what you want?"

Kersinski shrugged as if she were caught up in something beyond her control. "We owe this to the viewer, Mrs. Cooper. It really doesn't hurt a bit."

Chapter 22
Animal Studies

The pros stationed themselves along the rail while the cattle were settled for the next round of competition. Coy tied Money Honey at the back of the arena and tried to calm her with a few soothing words before he joined the others studying the cattle.

"I like that red heifer with the outline of Texas on her face," Cactus said after a few minutes. "She looks like she could find out what a horse is made of."

"How about that brindle cow next to the gate?" Coy asked. "I wouldn't mind owning a whole herd like that."

"She's got seventy-five written all over her," Cactus agreed, referring to an unbeatable score.

All of a sudden, Kenny leaned back and slapped the rail. "This is it," he shouted.

Some of the hands farther down shushed him. "You'll rile the cows," they scolded.

"This is how my people did it in the old days," Kenny said, just a little more quietly, to everyone and no one.

Cactus ducked his head away from the fence rail and looked at Kenny. "Say your daddy was a cutter?" he asked, surprised, because he thought he knew just about everyone who cut a cow in West Texas in the past fifty years.

"No," Kenny shook his head. "Not my daddy. Not a cutter. My people back a long, long time ago. I don't even know their names. They watched the buffalo just like we're watching these cows. They studied them hard until they knew what the buffalo would do no matter what happened."

"I reckon you're right," Cactus said. "Folks talk about the courage of Indians hunting buffalo, but I bet they used their brains more than bravery when they went on a hunt. Least the ones that came back did. I know I wouldn't want to take on a one-ton buffalo if I didn't know which way it was going to jump when I sneezed. Especially if all I had was spears and arrows."

"They had to be part buffalo to hunt the buffalo," Kenny figured. "They had to love the buffalo to know it so well. Just like you love the cows, Cactus. Isn't that right? Don't you just love those crazy critters?"

"I do love a good cow," Cactus said, doffing his hat. "Never met a true rancher who didn't."

"How about you, Coy?" Kenny turned to the other side. "They're something special, aren't they?"

"I guess you could say that after my sweet Linnie and after a good horse, I love cows more than most anything else I can think of."

"Hey, you guys!" Kenny poked his head through the rail and looked down the line at the other hands. "Don't you just love cows?"

"Sure I love cows! What do I look like?" said one man.

"Amen," said another.

"Got me a picture of one on my wall," said yet another.

"Shush!" the rest of the men chimed in. "You'll rile the cows."

It was about eleven o'clock that night when folks started saying things to Coy that didn't make much sense.

"You bring a box of cigars to pass out?" asked Todd Alexander as Coy rode out of the arena after riding turnback for Kenny and Lightning. Coy didn't know what to make of that. Maybe Todd had mistaken him for someone else.

He'd no sooner tied up his horse than Steve Beckbalm called out, "Coy! Why don't you bring me your wife's autograph next weekend?"

Coy lifted his hat and ran his fingers through his hair. What was he talking about?

Jim Garrison passed Coy on the way into the arena to ride turnback for the next rider. "I don't know if I would've ever told anyone, if I were you," he growled.

Coy looked at Kenny who shrugged. It was getting late and he was starting to wish he were back home. At least things made sense there once in awhile.

Chapter 23
Home Again

At first, Coy figured the county must be tearing up the roads again to make such a traffic jam so far out of town.

"You see any earth movers out this way when we left?" he asked Kenny who shook his head.

But by the time the Double C came into view on the next hill, it looked like every car in the county was coming for Sunday dinner. Nobody was moving, so Coy climbed out of the pickup and knocked on the window of the car in front of them.

"I've got a trailer full of hungry horses here," Coy told the driver, a man in his thirties.

The man looked at the woman next to him and at the two kids in the back seat. "I think we've got some potato chips left," he said.

"Why, thank you kindly, sir." Coy touched the brim of his hat. "But what I mean is, I've got to get my horses up to my barn over yonder, and we're stuck in the road here. Where's everybody going?"

The man picked up a newspaper and tapped it with his index finger. "We're heading to a place called the Double C Ranch," he said. "I guess that's where most of these people are going. Do you know if we're getting very close yet?"

"You could just about spit on it if the wind was right," Coy said. "What do you want to go there for?"

"We're going to see the white buffalo," the man said as his kids bounced and clapped behind him. "There was a big deal about it on TV last night." He cocked his head toward the back seat and added, "They promised to clean their rooms every day this week."

"And eat their vegetables," the woman said with mock severity.

"I'll even eat broccoli," the boy announced.

Coy turned white as Hope's hide. "Thank you, folks," he croaked, touching his hat again, but this time doing it as if he'd noticed a scorpion hanging from the brim.

He climbed into the driver's seat and stared through the windshield in silence.

"What's going on?" Kenny asked.

"They're here to see the white buffalo," Coy said, staring at the traffic jam and letting his fingers dance on top of the steering wheel. "Every last one of them is here to see the white buffalo."

"Who told them about it?" Kenny looked over his shoulder and saw that the line of cars now extended far behind them as well.

"Some television deal, I guess. Newspapers. Hell, it looks like somebody's got a white buffalo eight hundred number."

Coy pulled the truck into the oncoming lane—since nobody was moving in either direction it didn't seem to matter—and drove on past the traffic jam until he came to a cattle guard on the south side of the ranch. He pulled in and unloaded the horses so they wouldn't be banging themselves up in the trailer while he drove across country back to the house. Kenny saddled Lightning and led the horses back towards the barn.

A quarter mile from the house, Coy stopped and rolled down the window. "It looks like a Fourth of July picnic," he said to Kenny. "We won't have a blade of grass left after all those folks are done tramping around."

Coy parked and locked the pickup, saddled Doc's Patience and rode the rest of the way with Kenny and the horses. Money Honey started acting like a fool as they got near the crowd and Coy had to tug on her lead and sweet talk her to quiet her down.

A stream of children broke away from the mob and ran to see the horses. Coy's stomach knotted up on him. Bad things weren't supposed to happen at your own home, he thought.

"Can I pet him?" a red headed girl about seven years old asked, reaching up to Lightning.

"You'd best not," Kenny said. But that didn't stop her, so he lied, "He's got big teeth and he bites when he's hungry."

"Is he hungry now?" The little girl's eyes widened as she stepped back.

"Hasn't eaten since Tuesday," Kenny said. "His stomach's been a'growling all the way over here."

"Look out," the girl screamed, waving her friends back. "It's a biting horse! Look out! He's got big, hungry teeth!"

The kids retreated—some of them bursting into tears—as their parents ran to meet them.

"What did you want to tell her that for?" Coy asked as he yanked on Money

Honey's lead rope again. "She'll have nightmares until the day she dies."

"I didn't want one of these horses to step on her," Kenny said, feeling wrongly accused. "And, heck, Thomas Eagle showed me how to fix nightmares," he added for good measure.

"That's just swell because I feel like I'm going to have plenty that need fixing."

A plump woman strode up carrying a boy who was old enough to be walking on his own. "What kind of place are you running here, letting wild horses scare my children?" she demanded.

"Beg your pardon, ma'am?"

"This place has been nothing but pandemonium since the minute we pulled in the gate," she said. "Pure pandemonium."

The woman turned on her heel and stomped over the hill, leaving Coy and Kenny scratching their heads.

The crowd blocked the way to the barn. The men dismounted and began leading the horses slowly into the fringes of the milling crowd. "'Scuse us," Coy called. "Horses coming through!"

Before they made it to sanctuary, Money Honey whinnied and reared, sending the people closest to her stumbling backwards. "Whoa," Coy said, trying as much to calm himself as the filly. "Whoa, Honey."

Linnie broke through the crowd and Coy was never so happy, nor so angry, to see anyone in his life. She used strong language and elbows to clear a path through the wall of people. After what seemed like miles, they led the horses into the barn and closed the door.

Coy didn't even wait until the horses were in their stalls. "Ma'am," he said, so that Linnie knew right away she was in trouble, "I hope to heaven you can explain to me what's going on here, because whatever it is, I know there is no way on God's green earth it can be as bad as I think it is."

"Oh, Coy, don't you see the possibilities here?" Linnie searched his eyes. "This could be just what we need."

"What we need?" Coy stared in disbelief. "Like we need our pasture trampled into the dirt? We need our horses stirred up like a Mixmaster? We need all these strangers climbing around everything like some kind of circus?"

"None of these people have ever even heard of a cutting horse before, Coy. You're the only cutting horse trainer in the world as far as they know. We've got a million dollars of free publicity here."

"None of these people would know which end you put the oats in, Linnie. How am I going to train a horse here? I might as well try to make a living in Grand Central Station."

"You never can see anything you haven't seen before, Coy Cooper. Don't you know by now that the horses don't keep you in business? It's their owners who pay the bills. You can't live off an animal. Anybody knows that. Tell him, Kenny."

Kenny looked sick. "I guess I better put these horses up," he said, squeezing behind Coy with Lightning in tow. Then he turned around, looking thoughtful. "You know, lots of people used to live off the buffalo, Mrs. Cooper. Back before it all got so complicated. Back when folks still understood what was important."

Coy and Linnie stopped glaring long enough to drop their jaws at Kenny. "You're listening to the sound of young country," Coy said in a deep voice that belonged to somebody else, and they all broke out laughing.

Chapter 24
The Threat

It was half past dark before they finally got everybody bundled back into their cars and headed for the highway. After Coy locked the front gate, Linnie told him about the television helicopters. Linnie had been on every station for the prime time news, telling about buffalo, about how Wanda knocked down the fence to have Hope right in the front yard, and about how Coy trains champion cutting horses.

The commercials had barely come on before the telephone started ringing that first night. Linnie didn't know what to do but leave the phone off the hook so she could see what the other stations did with the story. As soon as she put the phone back in the cradle, the line jangled with calls from all over the world: Australia, Japan, the BBC, some reporter in Germany, and a guy who might have been Italian—anyway he couldn't speak a word of English and she finally had to say she was sorry in as many languages as she could before she hung up on him.

"It made me think about millions and millions of people that we've never met, who don't know you from Adam," Linnie said, looking at how the kitchen light filtered through the longneck Coy handed her. "And for a few minutes at least, they stopped whatever they were doing and watched something about buffalo and cutting horses on television. For a little while, they were right here at the Double C Ranch and this was the most important thing in the world to them."

"Aw, most people will watch whatever comes on the TV," Coy said. "That doesn't mean they care about it. A lot of folks don't even remember what they care about anymore."

"You're tired. You should go to bed."

"I'm not that tired."

"You always get cranky when you're tired."

"I'm not cranky! What are you talking about?"

"Coy, honey, if you had a horse that acted like you're acting, you'd know just what was wrong with it." Linnie pressed against his shoulder blade to steer him towards the bedroom. "How come you can't see it in yourself?"

Coy fell asleep even before Linnie had cleaned up the kitchen. The nightmares he had feared didn't come, nor did the exciting dreams Linnie had vaguely expected. They were too exhausted for any kind of dreams.

That's why it took Linnie so long to answer the phone. Through the thick fog of sleep, the sound seemed like the alarm clock, so she fumbled blindly with it for a moment before she realized the ringing came from somewhere else. She reached over to the night table and knocked the receiver onto the floor, then reeled it in with the cord like a fish.

"Hello?" Linnie mumbled, "Double C Ranch."

"Mrs. Cooper?" The voice came from far away, echoing out of a distant canyon.

"Yes?"

"Mrs. Linnie Cooper?"

"Yes, that's me." Linnie looked to see what time it was, but she'd knocked the alarm clock onto the floor, too. "Who is this?"

"I'm a friend, Mrs. Cooper, but you probably don't remember me."

"Who? What time is it?" The mystery stripped away Linnie's grogginess.

"Death," the voice said. "We'll be meeting again very soon, Mrs. Cooper. Sooner than you think."

Linnie sat up and snapped, "Who is this?"

"You'll know me when I come to see your white buffalo," the voice said. "Just remember, Death, Mrs. Cooper, Death."

Linnie heard a clatter, as if Death had trouble putting the phone back on hook, and then the line went dead. She tapped the switch a couple of times and said, "Hello? Hello?" but the caller was gone.

She nudged Coy enough to make him stop snoring, but there was no point in waking him up now. Linnie took a couple of deep breaths and eased herself back under the covers where she tossed and turned the rest of the night.

The next morning, Coy rode Doc's Patience down to the front gate when he heard Frank and Bubba honking their horn. He'd forgotten about locking the gate, and when he let them in, he paused for a moment and thought about locking it behind them. But the crowds were probably gone for good; it was the kind of a deal where television stirred people up for a day and lured them out on a little adventure.

Frank had another perspective. "It's a question of security," he said, looking out at Wanda and Hope's pasture. "You need to define a buffalo safety zone here so that your people know where they can and can't go and your buffaloes know where they can and can't go. Then there's no potential for problems.

"The latest technology for a situation like this is an eight-foot double-walled fence with razor wire over the top to guard against intrusion. Heavy duty I-beam uprights and struts prevent the buffalo or an unruly mob from using the bull-dozer effect to plow through the whole shebang. Isn't that right, Bubba?"

Bubba nodded.

"You haven't even finished fixing the cyclone fence in the front yard and you're trying to turn my ranch into a concentration camp?" Coy glanced at his watch. He didn't mind being polite to people, but it sure could suck up a lot of your time.

"Naturally, as an established customer, we can cut you a better deal—"

"Why don't you just do the first job?" Coy said as he gathered up Doc's reins and loped back to the barn.

Frank nudged Bubba in the ribs. "You've got to give me some help here sometimes," he whispered.

Bubba pursed his lips and brushed Frank's elbow away. "Yeah, yeah, yeah," he said.

The two men pottered around the downed fence for awhile until Linnie came by. "I get it," Linnie said. "You plant the fence seeds, fertilize them with a whole lot of bull dust, and wait for the fence to grow."

"Preparation is the key to any job, Mrs. Cooper," Frank said, holding his hands up as if he'd been robbed on the street corner. "The actual execution is the easy part." He looked at Bubba and clicked his tongue to prompt him.

"That's right," Bubba piped up. "We'll be done sooner than you think."

Linnie gave Bubba a hard look, trying to remember something. "What did you say?"

Bubba looked to Frank for support. "We'll be done sooner than you think, Mrs. Cooper."

"Well, just get on with it so we can get back to normal around here," Linnie said, as she walked past them.

Frank scowled at Bubba. "When will you ever learn to keep your big mouth shut? She might recognize your voice."

Bubba shrugged and pantomimed zipping his lips together.

They resumed their busywork for a few minutes until they felt the coast was clear. Then Frank took a pair of scissors from the toolbox and they stepped over the downed fence and began making their way cautiously towards Wanda and Hope. As usual, they stepped and stopped, stepped and stopped, according to whether Wanda's enormous, horned head pointed in their direction or not.

Their preparation for this job didn't include learning about the way a buffalo's wide-set eyes give it a pretty reasonable view of what's going on behind it. They did know that buffalo are notorious for shedding their hair in the summer, but they didn't have time to wait for that. Besides, the baby didn't look like it had much of a coat at all yet. They needed a color swatch right away for their plans to work.

Wanda let the two men tiptoe right up to Hope. Frank held out the scissors and, with his hands shaking, tried to lift a tuft of Hope's short, white hair to snip it off. Hope jumped in surprise and Wanda snorted. She shook her head, but the two men were gone before she pawed the ground.

Bubba made it to the truck first and collapsed on the seat, wheezing until he thought his lungs were going to flop out in front of him like a couple of fish on the river bank.

Frank jumped in, red as a cherry tomato, and slammed the door shut. He spread his arms around the steering wheel and hung his head.

"Sometimes," he gasped, clawing at his heart, "I wonder if we're doing the right thing."

Chapter 25
Stubby's Dilemma

Stubby Hitchins and Howard E. Gray watched the first news broadcasts of the white buffalo from different corners of the state. Both men leaned back in comfortable, leather chairs which the years had shaped to their bodies. Both men thought that the shows would reveal some essential piece to a puzzle that they struggled with. Both strained their ears to catch every word uttered by the immaculately coiffed, vacuous reporters.

Howard E. Gray didn't understand why he and Mr. Hitchins took time from their busy schedules to traipse all the way over to the Double C Ranch, only to watch some horse dancing in front of cattle. Mr. Hitchins hardly showed any interest in the white buffalo, which is where the real news value was.

Now if Howard E. Gray were a near-billionaire, then the world would see some insightful reporting. What a pity that a person with a nose for news, with a quick, intuitive grasp of all the intricacies of a situation, was given only a limited opportunity to get the message out, to sound the clarion. How ironic that those most capable of a job were hampered by those who made it possible!

Hundreds of miles away, Stubby watched all the news programs at once with Tiffany in his penthouse apartment. Like many of the world's great eccentrics, Stubby moved in unusual circles. His acquaintances included captains of industry and dock workers, artists and cab drivers. None of them knew quite what to make either of Stubby, or of his other friends.

But standing out from them all was Tiffany, sometime hairdresser and manicurist. Tiffany wore her own platinum blond hair in shaggy piles that erupted from the crown of her head like high-rise thatched huts. She caulked her saucer eyes with mascara and coordinated the glistening smudges of eyeliner to her lipstick, nails, and accessories so that she looked like an experiment from the crayon lab at Buford Elementary School.

While shopping, she sometimes confided in other women that God had told her to wear tight clothes. She would never tell that to a man, but then she never felt any need to until she met Stubby.

79

Stubby funded her sprees without flinching as she bolstered the Oklahoma chic section of her wardrobe. Tiffany's tastes ran from vibrant splashes of fabric which matched her color scheme of the day to the more traditional buckskin and feathers. The underlying theme was tight, with generous, provocative ventilation.

Tiffany stopped traffic and drew crowds. The first time Stubby took her to Caboosi's for dinner, she whispered finger care tips in his ear so that other patrons would not overhear her secrets. When the waiter poured her a glass of cabernet sauvignon, she cooed to Stubby, "They must like you here to give you a new table."

"A new table?" He looked at her blankly. "What do you mean?"

"I just stuck the first piece of gum underneath it." She smiled and lifted her wine glass. "Cheers!"

It was the first time Caboosi's violinist had ever been asked to play The Devil Went Down to Georgia; the first time anyone ever danced on one of Caboosi's tables.

Stubby thought Tiffany made an ideal companion because her zest rubbed off on him. He figured if people liked her, they would like him by extension. Plus her presence established that he was a nice guy, one who already had real friends and who was open to making new ones. Tiffany got to meet new people and clothes, and she appreciated the fact that Stubby was not possessive like some guys she'd known. Everybody was happy.

Ironically, the only thing that gave Stubby pause was the inner workings of Tiffany's mind. He didn't often drink hard liquor, but now and again he'd break out a very old bottle of bourbon and sip from it until midnight. Did Tiffany pretend to act dumb because it seemed to fit, like an old, reliable part of her wardrobe? Or was she exactly what she seemed: a simple, open, naive girl trapped in the body of a sex goddess?

Was that squeaky, lilting voice her own, or something she applied each morning like an ounce of rouge? Would she look and act the same if she lived alone on a desert island? For that matter, how would Stubby act himself if he were shipwrecked? And if Stubby and Tiffany were marooned together, would each of them finally find true happiness, without the trappings of money and the demands of society?

Stubby had an advantage over most men in that he wasn't interested in Tiffany's most obvious attributes. Their arrangements worked out well because neither felt a sense of obligation or possession towards the other. Each of them had cultivated something to make people like them—for Tiffany it was a frivolous sexuality, for Stubby boundless wealth—but had found that people might be attracted to the edifice, without ever knowing or touching the Tiffany or Stubby inside it all.

Stubby never quite came into synch with other people's expectations, like the way Mr. Gray thought Stubby was more interested in the cutting horses than the fabulous white buffalo of Coyote County. On the contrary, Stubby had invested a small fortune in Money Honey, but he was much more interested in the buffalo he did not own than the horse he did.

A veteran Stubby watcher could have told Mr. Gray that whatever he showed the least interest in was probably the thing he wanted most. That was as basic as breathing. Stubby could get the best deal when he bargained with someone who thought charity rather than desire motivated him. In fact, the only time Stubby's laughter rang with a note of spontaneity was when someone quoted him a price for some item in which Stubby professed scant interest.

Stubby's dilemma with the white buffalo was that he'd seen Coy, the hardboiled ranchman, shed a tear when he sold a horse he liked for five times what he'd paid for it. Stubby knew that under normal circumstances Coy would never put a price on something that he'd received as a gift.

But these were no normal circumstances. The mere idea of a white buffalo had inflamed Stubby's imagination. His heart had leaped into his throat at the first sight of Hope. That might be just a short leap in Stubby's case, but it flagged a passion that other men might direct at power, money, or sex—trifling things to Stubby's way of thinking.

Stubby knew better than to tip his hand by revealing his interest in Hope. He was not much good at lying, or even dancing around the truth unless it made people act as if they liked him. So his challenge was to make sure that the trail of the white buffalo would never lead to him.

Chapter 26
Insurance

The weasel-faced man with the bolo tie patted papers until they spread out over every inch of the big, oak kitchen table. He leaned back and beamed like he'd never seen a cloudy day in his life.

"We're the only firm in the entire Southwest with a special buffalo policy," he said, running his finger along each half of his short, bristly moustache. "Anywhere else you go, you'd have to have them customize a horse or cattle policy to fit your buffalo. Hellfire, a buffalo doesn't even look like a horse, how are you supposed to feel safe if you insure it like one?"

"I don't know—" Coy started.

"Well, I do and you can't," the insurance man said. "You'd be up all night worrying about it. Take the horns, for one thing. How are you going to insure your buffalo's horns against damage outside of normal wear and tear, if you're using a horse insurance policy? People try to take shortcuts, and they get stuck every time."

"I was going to say I don't know if we really need to insure this buffalo at all," Coy said. "What did you say your name was?"

"Merl," he said, sticking out his hand to shake for the third time in five minutes. "Merl Buchanan."

"Well, Mr. Buchanan, this buffalo didn't cost us a dime. So why should we spend good money to insure it?"

"Oh, oh, oh, Mr. Cooper! Sometimes I think it must be my own ears that are deceiving me. What is a life worth? That's the question we always have to ask. What price do we put on one of God's most precious creations?"

Coy rested his chin on one hand and drummed on a mound of papers with the other hand. A cutter rides into the show arena with a score of seventy points. It's what he does in the next two and a half minutes that decides if that score goes up, or down. Coy respected strangers. Any man he met started with a seventy and Coy gave him two and a half minutes to prove himself. With some men, the two and a half minutes seemed to stretch out much longer. Inside of thirty seconds, Coy could tell the only reason this man even knew what a buffalo looked like was because he had his first nickel framed on the wall of his office. "Hm?" he sighed in resignation.

"It's a very complex question," Buchanan went on, "and it's one that a lot of men want to shy away from. For one thing," he tapped his index fingers together, "you have to consider your investment. For another," he tapped off the next finger, "you have to consider your replacement cost. For another," he marked the third point, "you have to consider your emotional attachment. For another—"

"Hold on there, Wea— Mr. Buchanan." Coy placed his hands flat on the expanse of papers as if they were about to blow away. "You're going to run out of fingers to count on real quick. Now, we insure our good show horses because we have a lot of money tied up in breeding or buying them, in training them, and entering them in these big events. And Linnie and I have insurance because each of us depends on the other to get us through to the next day. But this little buffalo, it's a gift. It didn't cost us anything, and the way we use buffalo around here, it wouldn't cost that much to replace her if something terrible did happen—"

Buchanan couldn't wait, so he waved at Coy in excitement. "We live in a wonderful world, Mr. Cooper," he said. "But it's also a terrible world. There are people who will do terrible things for reasons that don't make any sense to us. Political extremists. Devil worshippers. Drug fiends. Do you have any children, Mr. Cooper?"

Coy shook his head.

"Teenagers, too," Buchanan added. "I'm sorry, but their parents will tell you the same thing I'm telling you. The thing is, all these people are running around loose. They line the streets of our cities, and now they're spilling into the rural areas, right here into Coyote County. It's a conspiracy of senseless evil and destruction. And you know what their target is? It's your helpless and innocent white buffalo. This creature will be a symbol to them. Television and the newspapers have alerted all these bad, bad people to the fact that something that's pure and innocent is right here at the Double C Ranch. These folks compete with each other to see who can commit the worst atrocity. I would guess that your buffalo is a target worth, oh, maybe a hundred points to them. Maybe a thousand."

"So, since something terrible's going to happen to this buffalo, and there's probably not a whole lot I can do to stop it, then I might as well make a few bucks off the deal." Coy stroked his chin. "Is that how it works?"

Reading people was the toughest part of Buchanan's job. Some people, like Coy, seemed to be able to go right to the heart of the matter and see the best thing to do. But sometimes—usually because they were a little shaky on the concept and they didn't want to appear stupid—people baited him and then booted him out the front door.

Buchanan wanted to say "Yes! That's it! That's exactly right! Now just sign here." But then he noticed how the corners of Mr. Cooper's mouth were twitching. He followed Coy's eyes to Linnie standing quietly in the doorway with her arms folded. She shook her head slightly and Buchanan realized he must look like a small woodlands creature caught in a bear trap.

"Have you ever seen what a mama buffalo will do to someone who messes with its baby?" Coy said, mercifully breaking the silence.

Buchanan cleared his throat and shook his head. "Uh, no. I don't believe I have, Mr. Cooper."

"Well, would you like to?"

Chapter 27
Ain't Superstitious

Kenny never would have described himself as superstitious, but he vowed that he wouldn't cut his hair until the Futurity. He wore his teal shirt every time he entered Lightning in a cutting. He listened to God Bless Texas on his Walkman every time he warmed a horse up for competition.

And he slept with the DreamCatcher on the wall over his bed.

The next time he saw Thomas Eagle, he described the way his recurring nightmare had turned into a wonderful, happy dream. "I can't believe the way that DreamCatcher worked," he said. "You should sell these things."

"If I sold them, they wouldn't work," Thomas said. "I thought you knew that much."

"Aw, why don't you lighten up a little, man?" Kenny felt cheated because Thomas didn't seem to share his high spirits. "Don't you ever have fun? Don't you ever enjoy life?"

"I enjoy life very much."

"Well, you've got one dang funny way of showing it."

"I'm glad you're happy. But you were only the hero of your own dream."

Kenny could see it coming from a mile away. "So what? Who else's dream could I be in? Anyway, Lightning was the real hero."

"Lightning was you, Kenny."

"You said before that the white buffalo in the dream was me. How can you change your mind now?"

"I'm not changing my mind, Kenny." Thomas looked as serious and patient as ever. "Each thing in your dream is a part of you. Your hopes, your fears and your happiness. Each part of you takes on a different shape so that you can see it for what it is.

"Dreams are slippery things. Sometimes a part of you will change into something else without warning. Sometimes the message of the shapes will leave you when you wake up. Sometimes a dream will come back to you after months or years if you haven't learned its lesson."

"What lesson? I just didn't want to have that nightmare anymore." Kenny felt like it wasn't fair that something so simple should be so complicated.

"That's what dreams are for. They're teachers. The dream world isn't something separate from this world where we eat and drink and fool around with horses." The corners of Thomas' mouth twitched upwards as he spoke. "That's where your spirit lives, where it comes out and tries to show you what your life means. It's fine to be a hero in your dream, but the dream is telling you to be a hero where other people can see it, too."

Kenny couldn't figure out what made Thomas Eagle tick. Kenny, whose black hair and piercing eyes were the only hints of his Indian heritage, had suffered enough racial taunts growing up that he could imagine what life had been like for Thomas, whose dark features could have been chiseled from the landscape of the American West. Yet Thomas never had a bad word to say about anyone.

In some ways, handling a horse seemed to involve a magic spell, like the princess who kisses the toad to release the prince. Anyone who showed a knack for messing with horses—whether he was a trainer, a vet, a farrier or whatever—automatically had detractors who would run him down behind his back. Yet Kenny never heard a bad word about Thomas who was so in tune to his clients that most people figured he was part horse himself.

The theory that Thomas was part horse might help explain his strength, and the easy grace with which his muscles bunched and relaxed as he went about his business.

Although Thomas was a descendant of the last Comanche chief, Quanah Parker, his interests and allegiance spilled over to other Native American traditions. "There's so much that must be remembered," he told Kenny, "and so few of us to remember it. Our people hunted buffalo in this country eight thousand years before Columbus discovered America.

"The tribe you come from is not the most important thing. An Irishman can become an Indian if he helps preserve these things."

"So what do you need me for if it doesn't matter if I have Indians in my family?" Sometimes, the more Thomas talked, the more confused Kenny became.

"You have it backwards, Kenny. You're the one who needs the past, and it's not because of who your ancestors were. It's because you've grown up in a time when everything's changing, when nothing holds still—like the herd of charging buffalo that Lightning galloped over in your dream.

"I'm not that much older than you, but we're generations apart. Your generation has an attention span like that!" Thomas snapped his fingers. "You wouldn't even try to train a horse if it couldn't pay attention any longer than that. Look at the television commercials that sell billions of dollars worth of crap to you and your friends—so many pictures tumble across the screen that one of them is sure to appeal to you. But how many people your age could sit and watch a sunrise without feeling antsy?

"You need the past, Kenny. I just hope you can find it before it's too late."

Chapter 28
Tough Going

Coy Cooper came from tough stock. His great grand daddy broke down his still, packed it on a wagon and walked from Tennessee to West Texas alongside his team of mules.

Coy's grand daddy, Cal Cooper, was eighty-eight when his horse yielded the right of way to a rattlesnake and left him in the dust with a broken arm four miles from home. The old man walked home, then drove into town, holding the steering wheel steady in his teeth every time he had to reach over with his left hand to shift gears.

The doctor put a cast on the arm in spite of Cal's cussing. He described the injury, and he told Cal all about the treatment required, and how long it takes bones to heal once the body passes a certain age. What the fool doctor couldn't explain was what good is a cowboy if he can't toss a loop?

Cal went home and grumbled a few days, but he couldn't get much work done at all. It's damn awkward saddling a horse when you can't bend your elbow and your fingers hurt just to wiggle. By Tuesday, he was fed up. He drove back into town and told the doctor to cut the dang thing off so he could get to work before he didn't have any work left to do.

"We can't take the cast off before its time, Mr. Cooper," the doctor said, gently steering his patient back to the waiting room. "Why don't you let Nurse Griffin drive you back home?"

Cal batted him away with his good arm and stormed out of the office. He paced all up and down Main Street looking for someone who would help him, but there weren't any good hands left in all of Coyote County, far as he could see.

At last he found Miguel, a kid who sharpened blades on a big grinding wheel in the alley behind the hardware store. He shook Miguel's shoulder to wake him up.

"You busy, young feller?"

Miguel craned his neck out and peered as far east and as far west as he could see. The alley looked exactly the same as it had when he started his nap. "No, sir," he said, turning a puzzled face to Cal. The old man didn't have any blades to sharpen.

"I'll give you two dollars to cut this dang thing off my arm," Cal said. "But if you cut my arm, I'll take two dollars' worth of your hide. You understand me?"

Miguel shrugged. He rattled around in his tool box for awhile. He finally came up with a hack saw that wasn't too bent or rusty, and set to work.

For the rest of his days, Cal groused to everyone who listened, "I got a good mind to go back to that fool doctor and get my money back. Look . . ." He raised his arm in disgust. "He put a crook in it!"

Coy got patience from his mama's side, but the pigheadedness came straight from Cal Cooper. It was a bad, bad combination, like getting a horse that was calf kneed and sickle hocked, both. Once Coy got an idea into his head, he could get stuck on it 'til the first frost in Hell.

So when the crowds started pouring in again on Friday afternoon, he told Linnie, "You brought them here, you can take care of them. I've got some horses I need to be training."

Only a few strangers had come since he cleared everybody out last Sunday night. But the scent of the weekend began to lure the white buffalo watchers back to the Double C. Coy decided he was going to just ignore the commotion and carry on with business as usual, thank you.

By Saturday afternoon the Double C looked like the midway at the county fair. It had everything but the Ferris wheel and cotton candy. Before long, the herd instinct had taken over and as soon as a knot of people got tired of looking at Wanda and Hope, they followed the path over to the arena where Coy was working the horses.

Folks who didn't know the difference between a cutting horse and a zebra formed little clumps around the fence. They shouted out questions and shot pictures on pocket cameras.

"Hey, mom, look at the cows!" yelled a red-haired kid in a tee shirt with a Holstein pattern.

"Can I ride your horse, mister?" pleaded a girl swinging from the third rail of the fence.

"Are these Quarter Horses?" asked a woman in a jogging suit.

"Mooo!"

"Hey, horse, come here!"

"Do you have a video for sale?" wondered a man in an Angels baseball cap.

Coy kept cool and paid them no more mind than he would the Futurity spectators who stomp, shriek and whistle every time a horse does something right.

He rode Doc's Patience right into the herd and cut out the best cow of the bunch. Then he and Doc fused into a single, mythic creature and the magic took over. No matter where that sleek, brindle cow leaped, Doc and Coy had it covered. The two beasts tested each other in a game they'd played before man had dreamt of saddles or spurs. They darted and spun, sending up clouds of dust that rose higher and higher on the sparse West Texas wind.

Coy had cut some good ones in his day, but this cow was a gift from the gods. He could have worked it forever, but finally he lowered his hand to Doc's neck and the gelding backed a step to let the animal rejoin the herd.

When he was done, Coy realized that dozens of strangers had lined the arena. Maybe they'd been watching in silence, or maybe they'd been screaming their lungs out; he'd been so absorbed that he didn't know which. But now he heard scattered, polite applause, and voices began to cut through the hubbub.

"Sir, is that a Quarter Horse?" the jogging suit lady asked again.

"Where are the rest rooms?"

"Can that horse run real fast, mister?" called out a boy perched on the top rail of the fence.

Coy heard the questions, but he didn't answer. Granddaddy Cooper was dead and buried long ago, but Coy heard his voice more clearly than those that filled his ears. "Don't cast your pearls before swine," Cal Cooper said. "Like as not, they'll just swaller 'em up."

Of course, Grandma Cooper used to say, "Don't pay any mind to someone who talks the Bible at you instead of thinking."

Coy counted off five deep breaths as he rode Doc out and went to get Money Honey. He liked people. He got along with people. He never felt bad toward a stranger without good reason. He liked people . . .

When he rode Money Honey into view, the crowd gasped. Adults murmured. Parents shushed their children. Kids called to each other.

"Mommy, that's a pretty horse," yelled a girl, and Coy felt the pride swell in his chest.

But before Money Honey could even enter the herd, her eyes widened until the whites showed. She humped her back like a bronc and Coy had to turn her in tight circles to keep her from bucking. The filly cocked her head in disapproval and side-scrambled over near the herd, sending the cattle shooting out in six directions.

"Mom, look!" yelled a kid who had seen a few things in his ten years. "It's a rodeo horse."

"Son of a big gun," Coy said under his breath as he felt a trickle of sweat make its way down his spine. "We've got some real work to do with you before the Futurity."

By Sunday, the crowds were even worse. Coy and Kenny had to plow a path through the people to get to the barn. Late in the morning, a Ford Bronco with the Channel Five logo painted on the side straddled the drainage ditch along the ranch road to get past the traffic jam.

A woman dressed in some television producer's misbegotten idea of western wear climbed out with a camera man. They elbowed their way over to the arena and watched Coy work Doc for a few minutes. Finally the woman poked her head through the fence and waved. "Hello, Mr. Cooper!" she called.

When Coy didn't respond, she turned up the volume a notch. "I'm Katie Kersinski, Channel Five Live. Could we talk with you for a few minutes?"

The crowd rubbernecked at the sound of her name. It didn't take long for those who had been milling outside of Wanda and Hope's pasture to come over and pack themselves around the arena.

"We'd really love to talk with you, Mr. Cooper. We're doing a follow-up segment for tonight's program on people's reaction to the white buffalo. It looks like you've got quite a show here."

Coy looked at her long enough to let her know he wasn't suffering from a hearing problem, then let Doc go back to work.

Undaunted, Kersinski shooed the people away to make a little clearing. The camera man set up a shot in front of the arena with Coy and Doc working the daylights out of a cow in the background.

"White buffalo fever has reached epidemic proportions in Coyote County," Kersinski said to the lens. "And it looks like the only cure is to come to the Double C Ranch and see the baby buffalo that has become the biggest tourist attraction in West Texas overnight . . ."

By the time Coy had locked the front gate that night, he'd missed the ten o'clock news—not that he cared—and Linnie looked as haggard as he felt.

"If I was not so dadgum tired, I would be madder than a snake on velcro,"

Coy said, slapping his hat on the kitchen table. "This isn't a ranch anymore, it's a zoo."

The phone rang before Linnie could open her mouth.

Coy picked it up. "Double C Ranch," he said in a voice as flat as a horse trainer's wallet.

"Mr. Cooper?"

"That's right."

"Mr. Cooper, my name is Andrew Parmalee. I'm up here in Fond du Lac, Wisconsin. You don't know me, but I saw you on the television tonight. My satellite dish picked it up."

Coy rubbed the back of his neck. "I didn't say anything to that television lady—"

"You didn't have to, Mr. Cooper. I'm calling because of the way you were working that bay horse while the lady was talking. Have you put a price on him yet?"

"The bay horse?" Coy looked at Linnie. "That's Doc. Oh, he's not for sale. You could stack dollar bills all the way up to a full moon at midnight and you wouldn't have enough to buy him. I'm sorry, Mr. Parmalee, I'm not meaning to be rude or anything, but that's my horse. He's going to be right here the day he dies."

Chapter 29
The Prickly Pear Prank

Folks called Cactus Gordon "Cactus" ever since he was a little kid. He loved to be a cowboy. He loved to ride. He loved beans and biscuits and cobbler. He even loved gathering firewood for the chuckwagon. But what he loved most was listening to the old hands talk about the old days, and the horses and cowboys they'd known, about the big storms and the droughts that never broke.

These were men who knew what cowboying was all about. They might not have seen an automobile until they were old enough to vote, and they'd never fly in an airplane, but they spent their lives perfecting an art that might never be used again.

At first Cactus thought they were all crusty old buzzards because he never saw them smile. But once he'd settled in and felt more comfortable, felt like maybe he was a part of the camp, then he realized that they were hardly ever serious about anything but the work at hand. Maybe they spent all those long hours alone in the saddle scheming, making up elaborate practical jokes to play on each other or on the foreman. Heck, even the rancher was fair game, and if it turned out he couldn't take a joke, there was always a big spread down the road a piece that needed a good hand.

A lot of times Cactus saw a man having a coughing fit after someone else told a campfire story, but it took him awhile to realize the coughing was a cover for his laughter. Cactus gave it a good bit of thought and decided there were several reasons why these men only smiled or laughed at night, around the campfire, when they could try to hide it in the shadows.

For one thing, their lives did not exactly lend themselves to laughter. Laughter is a social grace, and they spent too much time alone to cultivate that. It would be frightening to suddenly bust a gut laughing when you were alone with your horse on the plains, miles from another man. If you caught yourself doing that, you had good cause to doubt your sanity. Now, horses might enjoy themselves, but they never laughed. A man who did might look around at the raw, open miles and begin to think he was in the wrong line of work.

For another thing, the long, solitary hours gave a man time to hone a different sort of humor, a cerebral humor that didn't depend on belly laughs. A cowboy could spend days plotting a practical joke, getting everybody but the victim involved in its execution.

Back in the Fifties, Cactus worked with a man named O'Ryan who had a horse he called Little Red. Little Red was the best cutting horse in a couple hundred miles and O'Ryan was always finding ways to show him off a bit on the ranch, just to make sure nobody forgot how good he was.

One day O'Ryan came across a wild old steer down in the box canyon where they wintered the yearlings. O'Ryan didn't know where this steer came from, so he and Little Red penned it up next to a couple of big boulders so he could take a look at its brand. The steer had other ideas. He wasn't necessarily being mean, but he sure wanted to get out of that tight spot and his left horn gave Little Red a nasty-looking gash in the hip as he came flying out.

O'Ryan walked his horse back to camp about halfway ready to bust down crying. Little Red looked to be in pretty bad shape, but a couple of the men hauled him into town where the vet was going to patch him up.

Little Red had to convalesce at the vet's place for a few weeks, but every time anyone ran into town, O'Ryan had him check to make sure the horse was doing okay. The vet always sent back word that the horse was fine; don't worry one bit; you can't hurry healing.

Any of the men would tell you that O'Ryan was a good hand, but they couldn't resist setting him up. Slim Smith went to the vet's and put a beat-up old cart horse collar on Little Red and hitched him to the biggest wagon in town. Slim wiped shaving cream all over the horse's neck and sides and took a photo of the scene.

Every so often, the cowboys' work took them to a camp just a couple miles from town, so they always went in for a shave and a haircut and a sit-down lunch before heading back to the ranch. While O'Ryan was taking his turn in the barber shop, Slim ducked down the street and picked up his photos at the drug store.

"When was the last time you saw Little Red?" he asked O'Ryan.

"I guess it's near four weeks now," he said through a faceful of shaving cream.

"Maybe you ought to have a talk to that vet of yours. I think he may have some strange ideas on healing horses."

"What do you mean?"

"Well, look at this," Slim said, handing him the photo. "Poor old Red's all lathered up from working for that vet. You're the one who should be charging him for keeping the horse."

O'Ryan reached out from under the sheet to take the picture and practically got his throat slit by the straight razor as he peeled out of the barber's chair. He jumped on his horse and ran full speed to the vet's with the sheet trailing behind him like Zorro's cape before he figured out what they'd done.

Laughing was not permitted until much later, when the joke was recounted around the campfire. If you laughed as a practical joke unfolded, you might as well have said, "I can't top that one."

The more complicated the scheme, the better, because there was a certain beauty in watching an elaborate plan come to life and find its mark at the heart of the victim's foibles. Men might spend days plotting a joke while they rode the range. It was not unheard of for an accomplice to spill the beans to the intended victim, and for the two of them to twist the whole thing around so it backfired on the perpetrator.

There was one more reason why cowboys were not big on laughter. If a man found too much joy in the good parts of the ranching life, then the bad parts would surely crush him. One of the great cattle barons rode out with his foreman during the killing winter of 1918. They went for miles and miles past the carcasses of cows that had frozen or starved to death.

When he'd seen enough, the rancher turned to his man and said, "It's a good thing I'm a rich son of a bitch, because this would be the end of anybody else."

The hills and troughs of happiness and hurting weren't so steep for men who saw life go by in seasons, years and decades instead of day by day, the way other men measured their lives. They could call themselves plainsmen of the spirit, as well as the land.

These were the men who gave Cactus Gordon the nickname he would wear for the rest of his life.

The one thing Cactus missed about school was that he was getting to an age where he began to realize they had girls there as well as boys. The old hands at the Flying U Ranch could see that straight away.

A war was raging overseas, and folks back in the States knew they had to give up a lot of things they'd pretty much taken for granted. So Cactus didn't think much of it when he overheard one old cowboy telling another that the government was calling up all the extra steel in the country for the war effort.

A couple days later, another hand waved a paper at Cactus and said it was a letter his wife had written from back home telling about how every dressmaker in the country was busy sewing uniforms and blankets and flags for the GIs. A woman couldn't buy a dress for all the money in the world anymore, but most gals were making their own patchwork clothes now.

Now it just so happened that the manager of the Flying U Ranch had a daughter named Josephine. She was about Cactus' age, about fifteen, and she looked nicer than a pan of peach cobbler after a hard day's ride.

Cactus was still a little green to be punching cows all day, so one of his duties was to gather firewood for the camp cook. One of the men—probably old Murphy—suggested that he start gathering up prickly pears, too.

"What are we going to do with prickly pears?" Cactus wondered.

"Not just any prickly pears," Murphy said. "Now, you've got to find the ones with the real long spikes. See, with the war and all, women have to make all their clothes out of the ratty old things they've had in their closets and trunks for years and years.

"Well, that's fine, except the government's come around and gathered up most all of their needles and pins. All that's allowed until after the war is one sewing needle per household, and no pins at all. Heaven help the house with two women living in it because they'll be fighting over that needle all day long. Thing is, they need lots of pins to hold the scraps of fabric in place while they're hemming and sewing.

"Miss Josephine wrote to Franklin D. Roosevelt and told him that out here we have needles practically growing on trees. She volunteered to organize womenfolk in West Texas to gather up prickly pears and send them all over the country so that every woman in America can just pluck out those spikes any time she needs a pin for her dressmaking.

"Course, picking cactus is no job for a fine-boned girl like Miss Josephine, so you might want to help her out by gathering up some good prickly pears each day. When we bring them back to the ranch house, she'll probably get her daddy to give you a raise."

So Cactus rounded up prickly pears every day and put them in a big burlap sack that Murphy gave him. By the time they worked their way back to the ranch house, the sack must have weighed fifty, sixty pounds. Its dangerous fruit bulged in an unwieldy mass that gave a little guy like Cactus some difficulty. If he bent over and threw it onto his back, it felt like he was hauling giant porcupines. But if he held the sack in front of him, away from his body, his arms ached and he could hardly keep his balance.

Finally he dragged the sack all the way from the bunk house up to the ranch house. He stood on the veranda, knocked on the door and waited for Miss Josephine.

"I've brought you some prickly pears," Cactus said, by way of introduction. "They're the best ones on the whole west side of the Flying U."

"Why, whatever for?" the girl asked, searching back and forth between Cactus and the bag.

Confused, Cactus looked around and saw every man who'd ever punched a cow for the Flying U watching him from down along the fence. "Uh, I'm sorry, ma'am," Cactus mumbled. "I believe I may have made a mistake. I'm real sorry."

Before Miss Josephine could say anything, Cactus moved back to go down the porch. But the old burlap bag had been worn so thin that dragging it to the house finished it off. The bottom split open and sent prickly pears cascading all over the porch.

And from that day on, nobody could ever remember what name Cactus' parents had given him.

Some kids might have gotten all cross-wise over a deal like that, but Cactus didn't let it bother him. Heck, he'd seen cowboys a hundred years old, so he knew he'd have plenty of time to get back at every one of those sons of guns at the Flying U. The lesson he learned was there wasn't much a fellow could do about getting teased, so you might as well take it and go on.

And that's the story he told Coy Cooper when Coy asked him for some advice about what to do with all the people who were coming to the Double C Ranch every day of the week.

"They're not teasing me, Cactus," Coy said, thinking he hadn't explained the situation quite right. "They're getting in the way so I can't go about my business. I'm afraid there's going to be a wreck with the livestock and somebody's going to get hurt. They're upsetting the horses. They're driving Money Honey so crazy she won't even look at a cow anymore. How am I supposed to win the Futurity with a horse that won't look at a cow?"

"That's one thing you can't do," Cactus agreed. "But you're better off finding these things out now instead of later."

Chapter 30
Stubby's Agent

Stubby Hitchins didn't want to have anything to do with the white buffalo. That was the only way he could be sure they'd never be able to trace it to him.

Stubby could think of three ways to obtain Hope.

The simplest way would be to buy her. He knew that Coy Cooper did not want to sell, but he also knew from countless hours of playing Monopoly against himself that if you put a man in a distressed situation, all kinds of things become negotiable. Stubby could bring Coy to the table by threatening to build a shopping mall or a toxic waste dump next to the Double C Ranch. The downside to that plan was that Stubby would be the bad guy in a very public way.

The second way to get the white buffalo would be to stage some kind of a commando raid. A helicopter, a few gas bombs and half a dozen guys in black pajamas could have the critter out of there in five minutes flat without actually hurting anybody. That would bring more bad publicity, and even though it wouldn't be directed at him, lots of people would be unhappy. A better variation on the commando theme would be to panic everyone with stories of some terrible buffalo plague; make it look like the government was hauling Hope—and the rest of the herd—off to be quarantined. That would have a bonus in that the government would take some heat until things got sorted out and Hope was long gone. On the other hand, he didn't want to give the government a bigger axe to grind than it usually had.

The third, and most appealing, way to get Hope was quietly, to make it look like she just walked away. It was an elegant solution, since that's what buffalo used to do in the old days. An adult buffalo who wants to be on the other side is scarcely inconvenienced by a fence, so it would be easy to stage a break-out by Wanda with Hope following. Search parties would scour the county for a few days or weeks and then the whole thing would blow over. If the media played it right, the episode could be seen as a symbolic dash for freedom by the beast that made America what it is today. Unlike the other plans, this one could generate great publicity. Hope would become a legend. No doubt people would claim to sight her cresting a hill or drinking from a creek every now and then for years to come. The white buffalo would become the Bigfoot of West Texas.

And only Stubby would know where she really was.

But he needed some help to pull it off. So he asked Tiffany if she wanted to take a trip to Coyote County and pretend to be someone else.

"What should I wear?" she asked, snapping her gum and blowing a bubble that came out the same color as her lipstick.

"Something Texas. Something persuasive," Stubby said, shrugging. "Like always."

Chapter 31
The Proposition

The offices of Fine Fencing Company were located in a converted dry goods store that dated back to the days when Buford, Texas served as a hub for the people within hundreds of square miles. Buford had whatever the ranchers needed, supplies, news, services, recreation, or just a different set of faces to look at for a few hours.

The Fine Fencing Company offices looked like they hadn't been cleaned since the dry goods store closed during the Great Depression. Along one wall, cobwebs filled the lattices of roll upon roll of cyclone fencing. Pipes, rods and beams for fence posts rose between precarious stanchions, ready at the slightest vibration to tumble across the cramped walkway.

At the back of the long, narrow room were the desks of Franklin Fine, chief operating officer of Fine Fencing Company, and his associate, Orwell "Bubba" Fine. Frank and Bubba's geological filing system depended on a six to ten-inch crust of papers covering both desks. The order forms, accounts payable, correspondence, sweepstakes entries and comic pages from the golden age of the Coyoteland Courier had been periodically soaked by coffee and soft drink spills and misdirected chewing tobacco. In time, the arid West Texas atmosphere dried and hardened the papers. Then some new fluid soaked them, and they dried again, and so on until they had turned into rust colored papier mache.

This indestructible crust served as a foundation for a thick blanket of cigarette ash, dandruff, gunpowder, iron filings and common dust. In turn, this billowing outer cushion supported half-used matchbooks, prehistoric pizza crusts, shriveled apple cores and various cups and cans which were prone to fall over on the uneven surface, sending a new coat of goo down to reinforce the foundation.

When they were in the office, Frank and Bubba themselves were barely distinguishable from the debris surrounding them. The trained eye might pick them out because they were bound to the furniture by fewer cobwebs than most items in the shop.

Into this somber den of gray-on-gray, dust-on-dust, strode Tiffany, riding a pair of four-inch heels, her body testing the abbreviated flaps of crimson and orange leather that strained to hold it in check. The smart clap of her heels on the ancient, creaking wooden floorboards roused the proprietors from their mid-morning naps. As Tiffany drew near, Frank looked at Bubba, still bleary-eyed and slumped over the turmoil of his desk. He looked back at this appari-tion, this being from some distant planet, and he marveled that somewhere in the universe life could assume such a form, and he closed his mouth and swal-lowed.

"Mr. Fine?" Tiffany said, smiling and extending her hand as if concealing a joy buzzer, "My name is Stephanie. I've come a long way to see you!"

It took Frank a moment to find his bearings. He half-rose and shook her hand as vigorously as he was shaking his head. "That's right," he was saying. "I'm Frank. Franklin Fine."

Bubba made some kind of a choking noise.

"And this is my associate, Orwell Fine," Frank went on. "That's right. You can call him 'Bubba.'"

Frank straightened up and came around to the front of the desk. He lifted a rigid heap of papers off the folding chair, looked around, and added them to the strata on his desk. He picked up the chair and blew hard on it to send a cloud of dust away from this Stephanie creature. "Please, have a seat," he said, clanking the chair back on the floor.

Tiffany brushed the seat quickly and showed him her dimples before she sat down. She stared across the desk at him with wide, expectant eyes.

"Uh, yes. Welcome to the Fine Fencing Company," Frank said at last. He shot an annoyed glance at Bubba who didn't seem to have all of his faculties just yet.

"Thank you." Tiffany fished her compact out of her purse, snapped it open and blinked into it. "Oh yeah," she said. "You're probably wondering why I'm here. I'm here to make you an offer you can't refuse, Mr. Fine."

"I could see that the minute you walked in the door, ma'am."

"You could?"

"Yes."

"Oh." Tiffany opened her compact again before she went on. "I represent BB Enterprises, Mr. Fine." She leaned over the desk and whispered, "It's a very big company. Very big."

"And you need some fencing—"

Tiffany burst into laughter. "Fencing? Oh, gosh, no. But that's good. That's very good.

"Now, seriously," she went on, "We're licensing the advertising rights to the white buffalo—we call it 'Brite Buffalo Brand'—that was born right here in Coyote County not long ago. This thing is going to be big. Very big. It's going to be the next Nolan Ryan. Our clients, who pay a lot of money to license these rights, can use the Brite Buffalo name and image and this logo our artists are making. If anyone else uses that stuff, we'll sue their butts off."

Frank nodded. "That's very interesting, Miss . . . uh . . ."

"Stephanie," Tiffany said. "My name is Stephanie. Now you're probably wondering how you fit into this picture."

Frank couldn't stop nodding.

"We've already got what we call our first group of clients lined up. They're going to use the Brite Buffalo to advertise all the major stuff—cake mixes, motor oil, fashion things, lawn care products—all the big money accounts. Now we want to line up what we call our second group of clients—the ones who have things nobody would ever think about buying—"

"Like fences?"

Tiffany's face lit up beneath the hot wash of her cosmetics. "That's exactly right! Hey, you're good at this! Now, to get the ball rolling, BB Enterprises wants to offer you a six-month free trial where you can use the Brite Buffalo name, image and logo to advertise the heck out of your fences and just see if that doesn't do wonders for your business. You know what the women around here will be saying to you, Mr. Fine?"

"Why, no—"

"They'll be saying, 'is that a bankroll in your pocket, or are you just glad to see me?' Get it?" Tiffany looked at him, but she couldn't tell if he got it, and his voice seemed to be out of order again. "Anyway, we'll also produce a video for you to use to promote your fences. Plus, we will guarantee you—" Tiffany glanced at her compact again, "—guarantee you exclusive rights in your field. That means that no other fence company will be allowed to use the Brite Buffalo to advertise its products.

"Now, what do you say to that, Mr. Fine?"

Frank's attention had drifted. When he realized she'd stopped talking, he said, "That sounds terrific, Miss . . . Stephanie. You know, ma'am, I just couldn't help but notice how striking your hair is."

"Why, thank you. You know I majored in hair color at the North Texas College of Beauty and Fashion. Oh! That was before I started working for BB Enterprises, of course. This color is called Platinum Frost. You might not believe it, but you can get it right off the shelf."

"No kidding. You can buy—what? a bottle of dye or something—and make your hair that color?"

"That's right."

"How much does a bottle cover?"

"Why, Mr. Fine!" Tiffany rose, indignant. "Only your head!"

"Pardon me, Stephanie. Please, sit down. I meant how many doses do you get out of one bottle? If you had someone with a whole lot of hair, would they need two or three bottles, or what?"

"Well, I've never met anyone who needed more than one bottle, but I guess it could be possible. You're thinking of maybe a rock star or something, huh?"

Frank still couldn't stop nodding.

Chapter 32
Tourist Trap

By June, Coy had to face the fact that life would never be the same again. Along the road for a mile in either direction from the gate to the Double C Ranch, strangers hawked white buffalo t-shirts, post cards and stuffed toys. They offered souvenir spoons and coffee mugs, thimbles and key fobs, place mats and bumper stickers, all bearing pictures of Hope, or an artist's impression of how she would look when she reached maturity.

Coy couldn't come home without seeing agitated vendors who hollered and gestured at each other—now and then, they even came to blows—over who laid the strongest claim to the choice locations on the shoulder of the road.

Even when he turned into his own drive he couldn't find any peace. The Double C looked like Disneyland on the prairie. The crowds pressed and chattered on ground level. Light planes swooped low over the ranch like vultures armed with chain saws.

One time, he padlocked the gate during the day and posted "No Trespassing" signs, but he wound up feeling like a prisoner in his own home. It didn't work anyway. These human waves, families wearing sunglasses and plaid shorts, with disposable cameras draped around their necks and an insatiable craving for corny dogs, could not be stopped so easily. There was no way to turn back the tide.

Somebody told Coy he was sitting on the biggest tourist attraction in Texas that offered free parking and admission. Coy figured that made him the biggest fool in the state—in the whole dang USA—for putting up with it.

"Besides, I'm not offering it," he sighed. "They're taking it. Nobody asked me Word One about it."

"Law says you can shoot them," pointed out Buck Henderson at the Buford Cafe. Buck spoke with the authority of a jailhouse lawyer. He'd spent a year and a half—a local record—in the Coyote County jail. He did his time one night at a time, sleeping off three decades' worth of drunks.

"I'm not going to shoot anybody," Coy protested. "Besides, I'd need a machine gun and I haven't got one."

"Nah, you don't have to shoot them all." Buck waved his toothpick impatiently. "You don't even have to kill them. Just wing a few of them and they'll get the message pretty quick. They're not as stupid as you might be inclined to believe." Buck lowered his voice. "I know a man who can get you that machine gun."

The biggest topic of conversation in Coyote County was the goings-on out at the Double C Ranch. The locals couldn't figure what all those tourists were doing there, even though they'd been out to have a look themselves. They couldn't figure why Coy and Linnie didn't do something . . . call out the National Guard, hide the dang buffalo, start a rumor about some highly contagious disease, something. Who wanted to live like that?

The fact was, Coy was a soft touch. He had the patience of an old-time cowboy, a patience born of endless days on the range without the diversions most men required—drinking, women, gambling or television. That was a great asset when working with livestock and with absentee cutting horse owners. Coy had always found that if something bad happened or threatened to happen, he could wait it out and things would get better.

This was different. The whole situation got worse each day. Even Linnie was beginning to admit that promoting the business was one thing, but if you let it get out of hand, you might not have any business left.

All of a sudden Coy realized that the term "tourist trap" meant just the opposite of what he'd always thought. The tourists come and trap you, not the other way around.

He didn't know what they wanted from him, or from Hope. The Double C had become part of a Southwestern circuit. The RVs and station wagons arrived in waves, all sporting the same bumper stickers. People climbed out of their vehicles and greeted old friends. They talked about the last place they'd seen, and the next stop on their maps, either Palo Duro Canyon or Sea World, depending on which way they were headed. They looked at Hope for a few minutes if she happened to be around, and then they left.

Cactus had told Coy about how some of the Indian tribes used to wander the plains in the wake of the buffalo. In a way, these modern nomads were doing the same thing, except their lives didn't depend on the things that lured them across the country. Maybe it was a sense of community that modern life had stripped away that they were hoping to find somewhere in America's great in-between. Maybe Hope brought people together so they could recapture the things they'd lost, so they could share them with one another.

Unlike most natural wonders, the buffalo's unpredictability made it a problem as a tourist attraction. Wanda and Hope were just as apt to march over the hill, far out of sight as to pose for the crowds. For a lot of people, it didn't seem to matter. They walked around, watched each other, soaked up the ambience, snapped a few pictures of the family in front of Wanda and Hope's pasture, then drove off to pick up a few souvenirs and refreshments on the road outside the ranch. But there were exceptions.

Coy put up signs on the house and all the buildings that said, "Stop. Do not enter. No buffalo in here." The signs themselves attracted tourists. People formed a line leading up to the porch where they dutifully read the message, turned around, and walked back through the yard past hundreds of people waiting to clomp onto the porch for their turn to read it.

"What's up there?" Coy overheard one man in line asking another who was returning.

"Just a sign," he said.

"Oh."

At least the signs kept people from tramping through the kitchen, although they were less effective by the barn. Kenny and Coy could hardly saddle a horse anymore without first chasing someone out of the stall. At first Coy tried to explain some very basic concepts of horsemanship to the intruders (never pull a horse's tail, don't make sudden movements) to forestall a disaster. That had little effect, and eventually he contented himself with etiquette lessons.

"Ma'am, we can't allow smoking in here," he told a woman in a floppy hat and sunglasses.

"Oh, this is practically outside," she said, waving her cigarette expansively at the large open door. "There's such a nice breeze, I don't see how anyone could complain about the smoke."

"We really would rather people don't come in the barn because it bothers the horses," Coy explained.

"I can see that it would," she conceded. "Some of the people you have around here bother me, that much is for sure. Can you tell me where this buffalo is?"

"I don't know, ma'am," he admitted.

"You don't know?"

"No, ma'am. It's like that song that says, 'where the buffalo roam.' That's what buffalo do; they roam. They're large animals, ma'am. It's pretty hard to keep one from going where it wants to go."

"Well, I don't see how you can advertise a white buffalo if nobody can see it," she snapped. "Have you got unicorns, too?"

"We've never advertised that we have anything, ma'am, except cutting horses, but I don't reckon you came here to see them."

"You butcher horses here?" The woman put her hand on top of her hat, even though there was no breeze. "My brother-in-law is an attorney—"

"Calm down, ma'am," Coy said, feeling his blood get hotter. "We prefer to have live horses here. Cutting is what the horse does to the cows, not what we do to the horse."

"Does the Anti-Vivisection League know about this?"

"I don't think you understand what I'm saying—"

"I'm going to seek legal advice," she said, backing up until she stumbled into a man in a plaid shirt who seemed to be lost. "You just watch your step," she snarled at both of them.

On the other hand, many people were driven by generosity to visit the Double C. They brought Native American gifts to hang on the gate, things made from fur, feathers and beads. At first, Coy asked Thomas Eagle what these things were. Before long, he didn't need to because Kenny would report each day, "We got two DreamCatchers, a medicine bag, a bundle of sweetgrass and some tobacco yesterday."

"What's all that stuff for?" Coy wondered.

Kenny arched his eyebrow and said, "For Hope."

"Yeah, but what's a buffalo supposed to do with a DreamCatcher? I don't even know that buffalo have dreams."

Kenny rolled his eyes. "We do, Coy. Don't we?"

Chapter 33
Telephone Tag

II Hello, Mrs. Cooper?" said the reedy voice. "I didn't want you to think I'd forgotten you just because I hadn't called for a few days."

"Who is this?" Linnie asked after a moment.

"This is your old friend, Death, again," the voice said, cracking.

"Could you hold on for a second, please, so that the police can trace the call and throw you in the pen for the rest of your life?" Linnie winked at Coy.

"Sorry, I got to go now. But I'll be seeing your white buffalo pretty soon. Just remember the name, Mrs. Cooper, Death." The line went dead.

Linnie had been fielding most of the phone calls since word about Hope got out. At first the reporters woke them up at all hours, big-deal investigative reporters who couldn't even figure out it was two in the morning in Linnie's time zone. They called and asked her the same questions as the last interviewer, and as the next one, until she'd memorized a little spiel she could give these faceless people. She imagined them diligently scribbling notes in a cramped cubicle that might be in some exotic city, but it looked about the same as any other cramped cubicle anywhere in the world.

After the reporters came the calls from the people who had read or heard about Hope and thought, what the heck, you only live once, so I'll just call up this total stranger and talk to her about my views on buffalo or genetics or the fur industry or what have you. While the reporters were usually brief and to the point, the chatting people could go on for hours if you let them. Even so, it was hard to figure out why they'd called in the first place.

The reporters worked under the delusion that they were among the first to talk to Linnie about Hope's story. The chatting people always thought that Linnie was Linnie's secretary when she answered the phone. They shared a fantasy that Linnie and Coy were rich and getting richer as their celebrity grew, when in fact, the opposite was true.

Linnie fielded one more category of calls on a daily basis: the death threats. According to the Double C Ranch's telephone log, entire armies of frustrated buffalo assassins had been waiting for years for the chance to slaughter a white buffalo. It was a little scary at first, but Coy and Sheriff Burbank weren't too concerned.

"Maybe they'll all get here at the same time and kill each other in the cross fire," Coy said.

"You've got an awful lot of lonely people in this country," Sheriff Burbank pointed out. "They just want to hear you get scared on the phone because it makes them feel important. It's sad, but it's nothing to worry about. Unless you're a psychiatrist, I guess."

After the initial publicity subsided, most of the death threats stopped, but Linnie still heard from half a dozen regulars. She assigned names to the familiar voices. There was Garlic Breath, Cave Man, Secret Agent, Wall Street, The Kid, and Squeaky. Charting the terrorists' calls and looking for patterns became a strange kind of hobby.

Once, while Cave Man described to Linnie the terrible crimes he would commit, the phone clicked to signal a call was waiting. "Can you hold on for just a second?" Linnie said. "I've got somebody on the other line."

"Uh—uh—uh —" Cave Man had never been put on hold during a death threat before and he didn't know how to deal with the situation.

Linnie picked up the other call. "Double C Ranch. Can you hold just a moment, please?"

"Mrs. Cooper, this is Death—" said the reedy voice that Linnie knew as Squeaky.

"Yes, hello. I'll be right back." She switched back to Cave Man on line one. "Hello? I'm sorry, but I've got another death call here. Can I call you back a little later?"

"Uh—uh—uh —"

Click. "Hello, Death? How you doing? What's it been? Three days? I thought you found another white buffalo to kill somewhere . . ."

Bryan Bryson, who had given Coy the buffalo semen that produced Hope, called one night from Chicago where he was opening a shopping center with Byron the Bison.

"Linnie? Bryan. Congratulations! I just heard that you're a mama," he said.

"Hi—what?" Things happened so quickly these days that Linnie was easily confused.

"This white buffalo. Do you know how rare that is?"

Linnie sighed. "I do now."

"Byron and I have been on the road. I didn't know about it until today when a reporter started asking me questions about white buffalo."

"What kind of questions?"

"Whether I'd ever had one, and this and that. I told her how white patches are fairly common, but an entirely white animal is extremely rare. There were only records of seven being taken by white hunters. Different tribes had different feelings about them. Some thought a white buffalo was big medicine. Others were only interested in the value of the hide. They could trade one white buffalo hide for a couple hundred brown buffalo robes and a few horses.

"One wagon master even told how his oxen got loose, then came back to camp looking like porcupines on a bad hair day because the Indians mistook them for white buffalo and shot them full of arrows."

"How could they see well enough to shoot an arrow if they couldn't tell a buffalo from an oxen?"

"They couldn't see much of anything but dust when they were chasing buffalo. Some hunters said they couldn't even see to the ground beneath their horses when the buffalo were running."

"Let me get this straight," Linnie said, fidgeting with the phone cord. "The white buffalo was a big deal, but everybody wanted to kill it?"

"That's about right. I guess anything that's beautiful or different has some big problems when it comes to the human race."

"It's no wonder they're so rare," Linnie said, turning thoughtful. "And they've heard about this in Chicago?"

"Chicago? Heck, they've heard about this in Timbuktu."

The mailbag got a better work-out than the telephone. Coy and Linnie never realized how many far-flung friends they had until they began getting all these news clippings in the mail.

The stories all sounded the same. Since all the reporters extracted the same quotes from Linnie's monologue, she thought she could save everyone some time by condensing it, leaving out the parts the writers never mentioned . . . but then the story seemed choppy; it didn't make any sense.

Some days the mail box overflowed with letters from school children. Linnie opened a package with thirty-eight crayon drawings of a buffalo from Mrs. Stuyvesant's third grade class in Cherry Hill, New Jersey. "B is for Buffalo," wrote a little girl in Coos Bay, Oregon, "H is for Hope . . ."

"Dear Mr. and Mrs. Cooper," said a letter from Gary, Indiana, "I saw a picture of Hope and I think she is beautiful. I have never seen a real buffalo, but I would like to. If you bring Hope to Indiana, could you call me so I can come and see her? My parents will even take me to Illinois if they have to."

*

The Death voice that Linnie knew as "Squeaky" came out of Bubba at the Fine Fencing Company. Bubba turned to his brother and said, "I don't think this is working."

Frank didn't want to hear what Bubba thought. This buffalo business consumed him, but it sailed right over Bubba's head. First there was the simplest part, the sales initiative, which they were counting on to improve their short-term cash flow. Frank had delegated this to Bubba, the job of convincing the Coopers they needed a state-of-the-art security fence to protect the white buffalo.

Bubba called the Double C Ranch repeatedly and used his most threatening voice to warn of plots against the helpless creature, but he wasn't making much progress. "I say everything you tell me to, but I don't think she understands what I mean," Bubba whined. "I think she's making fun of me."

"She's making fun of Death?" Frank asked as he shook each of the Coke cans on his desk, looking for the one that still had some carbonation left.

"It's like she doesn't take me seriously. Maybe we should kill a jackrabbit or something and send it to her as proof."

"I'm glad our mother's dead so she can't hear you talking like this, Orwell P. Fine." Frank took a swig from the can he'd found. "Proof of what?"

"That she should be afraid."

"Ahh!" Frank waved at Bubba in disgust. "Do you mind? I'm trying to think."

The second buffalo project on Frank's mind was the video that would help their medium-term cash flow. This Stephanie lady had really sold him on the idea of licensing the Brite Buffalo advertising rights, especially since it wasn't going to cost them anything up front. Frank had seen enough of the pandemonium out at the Double C to know that this white buffalo business had a magical sway over people. This was going to be like having one of those big-name football players endorse Fine Fencing Company, except that they didn't have to worry about anyone flubbing their lines. They'd sell miles and miles of fencing, top-dollar stuff all the way.

Stephanie said Brite Buffalo Enterprises would handle all the details of pro-

111

ducing the video, but still, they'd probably want some input from Frank. He'd watched enough television to know what appeals to people.

But the third buffalo project, and potentially the biggest money-maker of all, was to figure out a way that Frank and Bubba could have their own white buffalo. The way Frank saw it, if the Coopers charged just a dollar a car load, they'd be rich enough to get rid of all those horses and cows and move to the city.

He'd seen some buffalo with white splotches before, so maybe he could breed a few of those together until the brown parts got canceled out and all that was left was a pure white buffalo. Trouble was, that would take so long before he hit the right combination. It would also cost a lot up front to buy the spotted buffalo that would be the foundation of the scheme. It wasn't easy, this buffalo business.

Frank ran his fingers through the sparse hair on the crown of his head. Those city newspapers were always running ads for hair transplant clinics. According to the before and after photos, they did some amazing work. Maybe if he could just find two of those splotchy white buffalo, he could haul them over to Houston or Dallas and have the clinic patch together one all-white buffalo.

"What about the other one?" Bubba wondered.

"The other what?"

"The other buffalo. The one that gave up half its hair to make the white buffalo. What's it going to look like after all that?"

"Who cares?" Frank wondered how a blood relation like Bubba could be so dumb. "Maybe it'll look like it's got the mange. Maybe it'll look like an overgrown chihuahua. What difference does it make?"

"So you won't let me kill a squirrel, but you're going to turn some buffalo into a freak? Maybe you're not so smart if you don't know that what goes around comes around, Frank."

"Ahh, shut up." Frank chipped away at the top crust of papers on his desk, looking for that city newspaper he'd gotten a few weeks ago. He knew there was a phone number in there somewhere.

Chapter 34
Fireworks

Before July, Linnie and Kenny and everyone else who ever met Coy never would have guessed that he had a temper. Coy never raised his voice, never turned red, never pulled his hair, never kicked a door.

If anyone asked, he would tell you he was mild-mannered for practical reasons. He knew for a fact anger and tantrums didn't work on horses because he'd run across plenty of hoarse, flushed, bald, limping trainers in his day. They'd all moved on to some other line of work sooner or later. And he couldn't see where that kind of behavior would do much to influence people, either. So what was the point?

He found out on the Fourth of July, as the thermometer crept near a hundred, and feelings ran even higher.

Coy felt like he hadn't slept since Hope was born. All these people coming and going were a pain in the posterior. They got in the way and made everything take longer than it should. They were slobs—funny how so many city people could talk your ear off about protecting the environment, and then scatter their pop cans and sandwich wrappers and cigarette butts all across the grass that was supposed to feed Coy's stock—so somebody had to waste time cleaning up after them each night. And when Coy finally got to bed, he worried, although he tried to hide it, about the danger. Sooner or later somebody was going to get kicked by a horse or run over by a buffalo, or a horse was going to get a tortilla chip stuck in its throat.

"If they ever make a movie of my life," a bleary-eyed Coy told Linnie on the morning of Independence Day, "it's going to be called The Curse of the White Buffalo."

"Oh, Coy, we're very lucky to have her," Linnie said half-heartedly. After all, she'd done her share of cleaning up and worrying. "Most people would give anything to have her. She's like a national treasure. Look at how much that singer offered us for her."

"He was no singer," Coy pointed out. Ace Duce, front man for the rock group Ape Linkin, had come with a limo, a stock trailer and a whole motorcade of folks who looked like they'd never seen the sun, much less a white buffalo.

Ace pulled the hair back from the sides of his face and told Coy, "I'll give you half a million dollars, man."

"That would be real nice," Coy admitted. "For what?"

"For the baby buffalo."

Coy looked out at Wanda and Hope in the pasture. Then he looked at Ace, who wore a leather vest over his tattoos. "What would you do with a baby buffalo?"

"I'm talking five hundred thousand U.S. dollars, pardner," Ace said slowly, without blinking. "I don't see that what I do makes any difference."

Ace and his followers left with an empty trailer. Coy had no regrets, but there had been a lot of times in the past few months when he'd thought it would make more sense to pay off the bills, have a six-figure bank account and return to a normal life than it was to be over-run by all these crazy people.

When Hope was just a few weeks old, before her hump began to show, a woman from some paper called The International Investigator poked around the ranch all morning before she marched up to Coy and said, "That's a calf!"

"That's right, ma'am," Coy said as if she'd pointed to a live oak and said, 'that's a tree!'

The woman squinted into a paperback book. "It looks like a Charolais calf."

Coy looked at Hope and laughed. "Well, I reckon she does a little from here. You can tell the difference when you get closer, but I don't recommend that."

"Why not?" the woman snapped.

"You can get hurt if you get too close to a buffalo with a baby."

"Are you threatening me?"

Coy jumped like he'd touched a cactus. "No, ma'am."

"But you don't want me to go any closer to that animal?"

"No, ma'am."

"That's what I thought."

A few days later Linnie came back from town and threw a copy of The International Investigator on the kitchen table. The headline said, "BUFFALOED!" in letters five inches high.

"What's this all about?" Coy asked Linnie.

"It's what everybody in Buford is talking about." Linnie sounded sick to her stomach. "This paper says Hope is a hoax. That she's a Charolais calf. That we're liars and people shouldn't come here."

Coy's face lit up. "Great!"

But the controversy only increased the crowds, the hassles and the insomnia at the Double C Ranch. To top it all off, the coffee percolator quit working on the morning of July Fourth.

"What do you mean it doesn't work?" Coy asked, staring straight ahead.

"I mean, it won't make coffee," Linnie said. "It just up and died. I think there's an old jar of instant in the cupboard."

"I am not going to drink instant coffee in my own home."

"You'll feel better if you do."

"I feel fine."

"Then I'll feel better if you do."

"Linnie, why do you always do this to me?" Coy wondered, still looking straight at the wall.

"I'm not doing anything to you, Coy." Linnie didn't feel cheerful enough herself to be cheering anyone else up. "Look, I'll go down to the road and get us some coffee from those souvenir people."

Coy slapped his palms on the table and pushed himself up. "There's no way on God's green earth I'm going to take anything from those people. They're the reason things have gotten the way they are."

"I wasn't going to take anything," Linnie protested. "I'm going to pay for it like anybody else."

"Pay those people? They should give it to you for free. They should pay you. They're like a bunch of bot worms eating away at a horse's belly. No better than that."

"Do you want some coffee or not?"

Coy let the door slam behind him. He stalked past the early tourists on his way to the barn where he found Kenny sitting in the shedrow, examining a rock.

"I found a buffalo stone," Kenny said, showing Coy the rock. "You see the head and the hump and the legs," he went on, tracing the features. "Thomas Eagle told me how a buffalo stone is good medicine. A man who found a buffalo stone used to oil it and wrap it every day. Buffalo stones used to tell my people if the hunt would be good or if the winter would be hard."

"Your people?" Coy looked at the rock in disbelief. "Kenny Rivers, I know for a fact you grew up on Houston Street in Buford, Texas and if anyone had told you your great granddaddy had talked to rocks, you would have poked them in the mouth.

"Is that rock going to help you get a week's work done? Because that's how much we have to do today, we're so far behind. Has everybody on this ranch gone crazy?"

Kenny stood up and felt his fingers tighten around the buffalo stone. He took a deep breath to relax. "I've been learning a lot of things I never knew before, Coy. Thomas Eagle says—"

"Thomas Eagle! Thomas Eagle doesn't know any more about Indians than Christopher Columbus did. He grew up in Buford, too."

"Well, so what? He knows about the stuff that came before him. The world wasn't made in a day, you know. A couple of things even happened before you were born, but you wouldn't know about that because you're too busy ruining Mr. Hitchins' mare."

"Ruining Money Honey? She's a head-wild thing that wouldn't even wear a saddle if I hadn't worked with her. Don't tell me about training horses because you haven't even read chapter one of that book, Kenny."

"Yeah, like the part about having your older horses do demonstrations for the new horses?" Kenny's fingers tightened around the buffalo stone again. "What chapter is that in?"

"Look, if you don't like the program, you don't have to work here. You can go hang out your own shingle and see how many horses people bring to you."

"At least I could train the ones I have how to cut a cow instead of throwing a fit."

"Go ahead and do it," Coy said, brushing past him, "because you're fired!"

"You can't fire me because I quit!" Kenny scooped up his saddle and stomped out of the barn, muttering under his breath. He bumped into a tourist on the way out. "What do you want to see a white buffalo for when there's a genuine psycho man right there in that barn?" he said to the startled man.

When Linnie came out to the barn an hour later, Coy said, "Good. I need you to ride turnback for me."

"Sure. Where's Kenny?"

"He's not here."

"I can see that. That's why I asked."

"Kenny quit."

"What do you mean, he quit? This is the only job he's ever had. He never quit before."

"That's the thing about quitting," Coy said, pulling the girth tight on Money

Honey, "you only get to do it once."

"Why did he quit? I'll go talk to him."

"Talking's why he quit."

"Talking? You and Kenny don't say ten words a day between you. That's crazy."

"Everything's crazy these days, so the sooner you start getting used to it, the better."

"Oh, you're impossible. I'm going to find Kenny."

"When you see him, tell him he better be moved out by morning," Coy yelled at her back.

Coy rode Money Honey into the arena alone. It just beat everything. This mare had more natural ability than anything he'd ever seen, but she was getting crazier every day. He didn't need anyone to hold the herd for him because he'd be plenty happy just to get her to look at a cow for a change, forget about doing anything fancy.

Sure enough, as soon as he put her in front of the cattle, she started prancing and snorting like he was taking her over hot coals. With the Fourth of July holiday, the crowd of buffalo watchers lining the fence swelled to twice its usual size. Folks yelled and waved so much that Coy—let alone Money Honey—had trouble concentrating on what he was trying to do.

That was when some yahoo tossed a string of firecrackers into the middle of the herd. The explosions erupted like a machine gun. Money Honey reared until her hooves scraped the sky. Cattle careened in ten directions, bouncing off the fences. They plowed into Money Honey who dumped Coy in the dust. Cows ran both ways around the arena fence until they met at the far side and charged back across the middle.

Coy jumped straight up, waved his arms and bellowed to scare them back before they trampled him.

When the cows had dashed back and forth over every inch of the arena, they began to slow down, and folks started clapping.

Some kid, too young to know any better, called out, "Are you a cowboy, mister?"

Coy stopped wiping the dirt from his eyes and looked around wildly. "Get out of here!" he shouted. "All of you get out of here!"

The people looked at him blankly.

Coy singled out one pudgy man draped over the fence and walked toward him. "What's the matter with you? Can't you hear English? Get the hell out of here!"

"Is this part of the show?" people whispered to each other.

"Go!" he screamed, turning redder with each ragged breath. "Go! Leave us alone!"

A few people began to turn away or shuffle backwards as Coy waved his arms. He picked up his hat, which was worse for the stampede, and poked at the crown. Then he threw it down and ground it into the dirt, with his spurs jangling.

"We don't want you here!" he yelled at their backs. "We don't need any of you!"

Chapter 35
Buffalo Hair

For a man trying to keep a low profile, Stubby Hitchins sure seemed to be fielding a lot of phone calls from West Texas.

Tiffany was madder than Stubby's accountants on payday when she finally got through on a crackling line from Coyote Town's Just Drop Inn.

"Why wouldn't you take my calls?" she demanded.

Stubby switched her off the speaker phone and strained to hear over the bad connection. "Did you call before? I told Doris to always put you through."

Tiffany snapped her gum just as the line surged back to normal, making Stubby wince. "I called four times and she always said, 'Mr. Hitchins in unavailable at the present time.' I know you're not busy that much."

"And you told her who you were?"

"I told her I was Stephanie."

"Why did you do that when your name is Tiffany?"

"You told me to come out here in disguise so nobody would find out who I was."

"Well, then how did you get through this time?"

"I told her I'm a friend of Tiffany."

Stubby felt his forehead for any sign of fever. "Okay, okay. So how's it going? What did Frank and Orwell think of your story?"

"You mean Stephanie's story?"

"Yes."

"They liked it just fine. You know what, Stubby?"

"What?"

"This is kind of fun, except there's not much to do out here except watch TV. Maybe next time you find a little job for me it'll be somewhere that something happens once in awhile. I want to go dancing or something."

"Tiffany, next time you come home, we'll dance all night. I guarantee it."

A lot of people wouldn't have entrusted such a crucial job to Tiffany, but Stubby knew that she was perfect for it. Before she majored in hair color at the North Texas College of Beauty and Fashion, she'd aspired to be an actress. She had to give it up because her range was so limited. For someone whose cosmetic flair pushed back the boundaries of fashion, if not decency, Tiffany showed a stunning lack of imagination.

But this role Stubby had devised for her was essentially playing herself. And Tiffany playing Tiffany was even better than Tiffany being Tiffany. As long as she thought the whole business was a game, things were okay. And in a way, it was a game.

Not long after Tiffany's call, Doris buzzed to say that a Mr. Kenny Rivers was on the line. Maybe Doris was slipping. First she shrugged off calls from Tiffany, whose squeaky voice gave her an unforgettable ID, and now she was giving some guy Stubby had never heard of the chance to get through. There were men on Wall Street who would give up their first born for a chance to talk to Stubby.

"Do I know this guy?" Stubby asked Doris over the intercom.

"He says that you don't, Mr. Hitchins."

Alone in his sprawling office, Stubby nodded. "Do you think I should talk to him?"

"Yes, sir. It's about your cutting horses."

Stubby's standing orders told Doris to put through calls from anyone who wanted to talk about cutting horses. Venture capitalists, entrepreneurs with the deal of a lifetime, and government investigators had little chance of talking to B.K. Hitchins Jr. That fell into the realm of business.

Cutters shared a secret so great and deep it might have been mistaken for an instinct. They knew that when the magic flowed through the right horse, the world's illusions fell away in chunks.

And it was fun.

Cutting was like a drug. It took normal, everyday people and turned them into twitching addicts whose lives revolved around their next chance to climb in the saddle and face a cow. Cutters didn't care whether Stubby was a billionaire or a bumpkin, as long as he talked horses. For Stubby, that subculture was doubly rewarding because he could shed the trappings of his wealth and be accepted for that tiny part of him that had been locked inside all those years, the cowboy.

"Mr. Rivers," he said brightly, "what can I do for you today?"

"Mr. Hitchins, you don't know me, but you sure have been helping me out, and I wanted to thank you."

"You're welcome," Stubby said automatically.

"I used to work for Coy Cooper at the Double C Ranch out here in Coyote County, and he told me you were making the Futurity payments for all of the three-year-olds on the place. Like I say, Mr. Hitchins, I don't work at the Double C anymore, and I'm nothing but a poor boy, but I sure would like to keep my horse paid up in that Futurity, because I do believe I've got the winner."

"Now, if you've been working at the Double C, you must know that my mare, Money Honey, is there with Coy Cooper." Cutting was the one field in which Stubby allowed himself a show of pride. "Some folks say they think old Money has a pretty good shot at winning."

"She's sure enough a good mare, Mr. Hitchins, and she'll make you a real fine broodmare one day, but the fact is . . . uh . . ."

"What?"

Kenny didn't know exactly how to tell a man that his horse was being wasted. It was like letting him know his wife was running around on him. Kenny took a deep breath. "The fact is, I know everything that's been going on at the Double C. Everything's all messed up with this white buffalo business."

Stubby didn't say anything for a long moment as he wondered what went wrong. Had Tiffany tipped her hand? Was the buffalo-napping scheme in danger? Stubby hadn't been blackmailed since he was a ten-year-old with stolen cookies weighing on his conscience, but this sounded like the routine. "So, Kenny—can I call you Kenny? Do you need some help keeping your horse paid up in the Futurity?"

"I'd give you half of what she wins in the Futurity," Kenny said quickly.

Stubby pulled the phone away from his ear and screwed up his eyes at it. Honest people make such lousy crooks, he thought. "Let's say ten percent, Kenny."

"Gee, Mr. Hitchins, I don't know if I can afford to give up that much . . ."

"No, no. I get ten percent of what she wins. You get to keep ninety percent."

*

Everyone kept the phone lines buzzing out of Coyote County. In an arduous series of calls, Frank Fine worked his way up the switchboard ladder to the senior vice president of marketing at Patched Thatch, Inc., which billed itself as the Southwest's leading hair transplant clinic.

But even after he got through, he still had trouble making the man understand what he wanted.

"We transplant human hair," the veep said. "I don't think you'd have much success transplanting buffalo hair from a cosmetic point of view. And frankly, I'm not sure that your scalp wouldn't reject it. Plus, that might put our license in jeopardy. We're sworn to uphold very strict standards."

"Oh, no, no, no. I don't want to transplant buffalo hair to my head," Frank tried again. "I want to transplant it to another buffalo—"

The vice president switched the speaker phone on so it sounded like he lived in a huge cavern. "I've never heard of a buffalo going bald," he said. "Maybe you'd be better off putting some kind of sweater on it to keep it warm, if that's what you're worried about. Find a nice brown mohair and you probably couldn't even tell the difference. At least not from as close as you'd want to get to a buffalo with a hair problem."

"What's that noise?" Frank demanded.

"What noise?"

"It sounds like someone's trying not to sneeze."

"Oh, we've got a bug going around the office," the vice president's voice said between ragged breaths.

Frank finally hung up in frustration and found Bubba staring at him expectantly.

"Idiots!" Frank growled. "He said the best bet would be to have a toupee custom made."

"That would be a lot of work," Bubba decided after a minute. Finding an easier way was the very foundation of the Fine Fencing Company. That philosophy held sway over all other considerations, even generating income. You could go a long way on debt, so what good was money if it took too much effort?

Bubba took the phone and made a death threat to the Double C Ranch while Frank cussed and fumed in the background. Frank could hardly wait for that Stephanie girl to come back. He looked forward to her appearances anyway. She came over often with a case full of contracts or video scripts and transformed the cramped and dingy world headquarters of the Fine Fencing Company into a palace of color and anticipation.

"You know, big brother, that Stephanie woman's never going to give you a tumble," Bubba said when he'd finished terrorizing Linnie. "I bet she sashays like that every time there's a man within two miles of her."

Frank's stare went through his brother, through the precarious stack of half-used paint cans, through the wall. "Maybe back in the city, where men are stacked up like cord wood," he admitted. "But you can't be blamed for not having much female know-how. See, a woman that's all penned up there in Coyote Town is going to be missing the attentions of the masculine persuasion, if you know what I mean. You notice how each time she comes in here there's a little more 'sash' in her sashay? That's what I'm talking about, and you'd best pay some mind."

Frank took some pride in having convinced the Stephanie gal to throw twenty-four twelve-ounce bottles of Platinum Frost hair color into the deal. She might be a city slicker, but when he turned on his country charm, he could win over anyone of the feminine gender. They made Bubba carry the carton in from the trunk of her BMW.

"I don't mean to get personal, Mr. Fine," Tiffany said, "but I couldn't help noticing that your hair might not be as thick around the top as it used to be. Hair coloring is kind of like money, you know—you can't take it with you. Now, I know a strong and sturdy man like yourself has a lot of years left, but . . . uh . . . do you mind my asking what you're planning to do with all this?"

"Can you keep a secret?" Frank leaned so close to her bangled ear that he nearly swooned from the clouds of grape and patchouli that wafted off of her.

"Sure. I was the first one to find out that Margaret Rosewell's baby didn't belong to her husband. Do you know Margaret? She's one of those fa-fa Dallas ladies. I used to do her hair before I got into the buffalo business."

Frank backed away, his eyes large as fencing pipe.

"It's okay," Tiffany went on. "Everybody knows now. I never told anyone while it was still a secret."

"Oh." Relieved, Frank closed in on her again. "If the truth be told, Miss Stephanie, we're going to dye a buffalo white."

Tiffany's mouth fell open. She craned her neck back to get a good look at him, and then she burst out laughing. "Okay, so don't tell me. You guys are really something, you know that? You're really something."

"Miss Stephanie, I swear on a bible that's what we're going to do. Isn't that right, Bubba?"

Bubba hummed as he nodded.

"You guys! Is this really a secret? I can't wait to tell Julie back home."

Frank pressed his index finger to her lips and shook his head. "Top secret. It's a government project. They do all their buffalo research out here. Real hush-hush stuff."

"Oh!" Tiffany became very serious. "I'll do anything I can to help."

Chapter 36
Alligator Skins

Coy looked and felt more like a zombie than a cowboy. This white buffalo business had worn him out and he had a hard time smiling at people.

"You look troubled," said Long Feather, who had visited the ranch repeatedly since the spring when his niece, Nancy McDonald, told him about the white buffalo.

"I guess I am," Coy admitted. "Seems like everything else that's ever happened, a fellow could do something about it. But this is different. All these people, day and night, tearing away at me. I don't know what to do, and there's just not much left of me."

Coy paused and touched Long Feather's shoulder. "I didn't mean you, partner. You and your friends are doing something you believe in, something that's important to you.

"It's these other people who are here because they don't believe in anything . . . or they don't know what to believe in. Those are the ones who are driving me crazy."

Long Feather looked at him a long time before he said, "Maybe their reason for being here isn't what you or they think it is at all. A flower might make a thousand seeds to produce one more flower, and all around it the bluejays are getting fat."

Coy was too tired to figure out riddles. All he knew was he had stretched himself pretty thin by the time he called Cactus Gordon.

"I had to let Kenny go, so I'm a little short handed here now, Cactus. I've got to find a young guy pretty quick who knows which end of a horse to put the hay in."

Cactus usually had a quick answer to any question, whether it concerned cutting horses or culture, but there was a long silence before he said, "I thought Kenny was a pretty good young hand."

"Aw, he figured he knew just about everything that a man needed to know. I was afraid he'd scare the horses with his head swelled up like that."

"That's just because he's young," Cactus said quickly. "I seem to recall another man who was a lot smarter when he was twenty-two than he is today. Trouble is, he hasn't seen how many ways things can go wrong yet. That makes the world a lot less complicated than an old geezer like me or you might think it is. It's a tough job being patient when you know that things can get done just like that." He snapped his fingers.

"You don't need another helper, you need to work with what you've got," Cactus went on. "It's like getting a sour cow in the finals. You just have to ride it out."

"Well, Kenny's the one who's ridden out, so I need to find somebody to give me a hand around here. Fact is, I need an army, what with all these people hanging around to see the buffalo all the time. And on top of it all, Money Honey is going straight backwards. By next week, she'll be spooking at her own shadow."

"First you need to know what's scaring her," Cactus said.

"She's always been a little crowd shy and I hate to say it, but this ranch is more crowded than a snake hole at sundown."

"You know, Coy, I bet I could find ten guys who'd like to swap problems with you."

"Why's that?" The words were so short they even startled Coy who always had time for Cactus.

"Because not many fellows are lucky enough to have problems and answers all rolled into one."

"What do you mean?"

"She's afraid because she doesn't know what a crowd is, just like you and me might be afraid of dying because we don't really know what that is. You make that mare take a good, long look at the thing that's got her all wound up and she'll see that there's no sense fussing about it."

"Well, you could show me a dead person every day and I don't know that I'd be any happier thinking what it would be like if it was me."

"That's because you're looking at a dead thing, not death," Cactus said. "You know, when I had my operation, I was plenty scared before hand even if those doctors said I didn't have anything to worry about. Hell, doctors couldn't charge so much if some of their people didn't die.

Cactus nodded at a gelding in the warm-up ring. "There's one healthy horse. It's shining like a penny straight from the bank he said. "Anyway, while they were filling me up with knock-out gas and pumping all that blood through me,

125

I looked around and saw myself down there, all carved up on that table like a Christmas turkey. And all of a sudden, I wasn't scared anymore. I was closer to being dead than I'd been since the time Old Red chased that wild steer right over the edge of the cliff, back when I was sixteen years old at the Flying U.

"But it didn't matter anymore. I watched those doctors a'pounding away at me and I knew that if I didn't die this time, I would some other time. Me and death were just getting close enough to sniff each other, so we won't have any misunderstandings when the time comes."

"That's very interesting, Cactus, but how's it going to help me train my horse?"

"Now, Coy, if you don't think training horses is easier than dying, then you may be in the wrong business entirely."

The thing about Cactus was he never laughed when he was teasing you, but he sure would later when he was telling other folks about it.

"Those old boys over in Louisiana love to match their horses even more than they love a bowl of gumbo," Cactus went on. "Always have. And they don't mind betting a dollar on the deal, either. Now, I don't know if it's the money or the pride that counts for more, but some folks will do some funny things to win a race.

"Sometimes an old boy will be so intent on winning that he'll hang alligator skins all over his barn."

"Alligator skins?" Coy could get so wrapped up in one of Cactus' stories that he'd forget his problems for awhile.

"Even a horse that's never seen nor heard of an alligator is afraid of them. I guess they smell so nasty that a horse figures one would eat you up right from the get-go. So this old boy raises his horses with alligator skins hanging around it every day of its life and after awhile the horse doesn't pay it no mind. That's just as much a part of training a Louisiana race horse as legging it up and rubbing it down."

Cactus studied Coy's face before he went on, "So the night before the race, the old boy sends someone out to the track to rub alligator skins all over the starting gates. Next morning, the old boy's horse feels right at home, but the horse he's running against isn't used to that smell and it makes him nuttier than a pecan pie. The poor horse'll be jumping out of his skin, trying to see what's making that nasty, horse-eating smell. And here the old boy's horse is already a hundred yards in front before the scared horse knows there's a race going on.

126

"There's a lesson for you and Money Honey in there. You just let her get used to all those noisy people, and she'll start thinking about the job she has to do instead of who is watching her do it."

Chapter 37
Cow Culture

Linnie picked a magazine at random from the rack in Dr. Hefflefinger's waiting room. A subscription card made it fall open to a photo feature about a new hairstyle that was sweeping the nation.

"Buffalo Do!" screamed the headline. "Inspired by a rare white buffalo born in West Texas, the new look appeals to women who don't want to get lost in the herd."

The pictures showed New York City models, celebrity teens in California, and the Springfield avant garde, all sprouting billows of garish, bleached hair.

"Bison chic puts me in touch with America's past," said one of the women, "but lets me be as modern as tomorrow."

"It's just fun," admitted another. "You can throw away your hair care rule book."

Linnie felt the knot in her stomach tighten, but she couldn't put the magazine down. When the nurse led her to the examining room, Linnie carried the magazine with her.

"What seems to be the problem, Mrs. Cooper?" the doctor asked, squinting at his clipboard.

"This!" she snapped, tossing the magazine down. "This is the problem. I can't sleep. I can't eat. My husband and I have been married eight years and all of a sudden we can't get along with each other. Our business is falling apart. I have chest pains and sinus problems. I feel a fist that won't quit wringing out my guts like a sponge. That's it for starters."

Dr. Hefflefinger didn't look away from his clipboard. "Mm-hm? Have you been under any stress lately? Bills mounting up? Family trouble? Anything unusual going on in your life at the moment?"

Linnie wanted to send a form letter to every district attorney in the United States of America: if they needed an impartial juror, someone oblivious to any amount of pre-trial publicity, no matter how outrageous, here was their man.

Once Linnie's life had seemed that simple. She'd been a hustling up-and-comer in the marketing department for a glassware company. Her life bounced from one trade show to another. The press releases, media events and Rolodex cards blurred together in frantic confusion. The job left her breathless, but if she could just set aside a week, maybe just three days, she could regroup, get organized, feel like she could cope with it all.

She'd been there two and a half years when her boss called her into his office one spring day. A few junior executives were taking their key people to a three-day retreat in West Texas.

"What's in West Texas?" Linnie asked in all seriousness, but she broke out laughing before he replied as she imagined all kinds of answers, none of which sounded like a good reason to go there.

"Cactus Gordon's Cow Culture College," he said.

"What? A dude ranch?" Linnie couldn't imagine the company footing the bill for anything that sounded like real fun.

Cactus was nobody's fool. He loved ranching, but he knew that a few cents a pound on the hoof either way spelled the difference between success and failure. He could still load a horse in the trailer and pick up a decent check at any weekend cutting horse show. But he knew that the cowboy experience was worth more than cowboy skills in this day and age.

So what if primary industry took a beating? Cactus could cash in by giving businessmen saddle seminars where they learned how a plainsman's philosophy could make them successful in their own fields.

Individualism, industriousness and integrity were the cornerstones of his program. He called it "The Three I's" so they wouldn't forget, and also because these people got nervous if you talked about things that they couldn't count.

"We raise cattle here, but we're not going to feed you any bull," Cactus always said during his opening remarks. "We figure you know all about bull already." They loved him.

"A man's got to make sure his windmills work and his fences stand," Cactus told them. These business people were bright in their own way. He hardly had to say anything more before they started jotting notes about "auditing resources and maintaining infrastructure." Fact is, he just had to tell them what he learned in his first week on the Flying U all those years ago, let them ride a horse, and sit back and collect enough money to keep his herd growing every year.

If Cactus wanted to take a nap or have some fun, he let the people catch and saddle their own horses. That taught them more about labor relations than they ever learned while getting their MBAs.

Cactus took these business people out of their element so they had no power and they had to pay attention. Then he introduced them to his way of looking at things, and that was about all he needed to do. It was kind of like bringing a horse in from the herd and breaking it. You didn't need that bucking bronco stuff that a lot of city people imagined. You just worked with the horse nice and gentle until it was thinking the way you were thinking.

Coy had recently left Cactus to go out on his own, but everyone who had ever worked for Cactus enjoyed coming back for one of his Cow Culture sessions. Coy could just be himself and these people with creases in their blue jeans would ask him questions like they thought he was some kind of professor of the plains.

"Do you talk to your horse?" asked a young man from the glassware company's public information department.

"I guess every cowboy ever born does," Coy admitted. "It's kind of funny because some of them never talk to their horse if there's someone else around who might hear them. And some of them only talk to their horse if there's nobody around who might hear them. But the way you tell a real cowboy is if he listens to his horse."

While Linnie's colleagues were falling in love with Cow Culture College, Linnie was falling in love with a cowboy. Coy seemed as fresh as the West Texas air compared to the pretensions and the sense of urgent folly that ruled her career. It wasn't part of the job, but Coy could listen to a woman at least as well as he listened to his horse.

The lesson Linnie learned in those few days, the lesson that changed everything she knew, was that life didn't have to be so complicated. All of these problems and pressures, all of these great weights were just things we had done to ourselves. You could hoist them on to a shelf, lock the door and walk away. You could move to West Texas, marry a cowboy with a good heart, and never worry about pleasing anyone else because if you pleased yourself, then you'd done a good job by who you are.

Linnie had walked away from life's complications eight years ago.

And now they'd finally tracked her down to the Double C Ranch.

Chapter 38
The Green Buffalo

The cheapest buffalo Frank could find was a flea-bitten old steer named Homer that had spent the last several years in the "look but don't touch" section of a roadside petting zoo over in Cornwell County.

Homer tipped the scales right around sixteen hundred pounds and Frank told Bubba that he was going to be worth his weight in ten-dollar bills. Bubba thought several minutes before asking, "How many ten-dollar bills are there to a pound?" He fell silent again when he saw the warning look on Frank's face.

Frank and Bubba shared a small clapboard house on a roomy lot a couple of blocks from the Fine Fencing Company's world headquarters in Buford. An immaculate picket fence surrounded the property, but they were lax enough about mowing the lawn that there would be a few days' worth of grazing available for their guest.

As a futile gesture, they tethered Homer in the backyard. It was futile because Homer could pull up the stake and walk through the fence anytime he wanted, but as long as the grass held out, he had no reason to leave.

Frank stepped around to the front of the house for just a minute while Bubba turned the garden hose on Homer, but he needn't have worried. The buffalo jumped at the first spray, but then welcomed the cool jet of water. Homer pitched his head and wiggled his butt.

A timid Bubba approached Homer and dabbed his flank with a sponge dipped in Self-Bleaching Platinum Frost hair coloring. When Homer remained indifferent, Bubba became bolder and he spent the rest of the afternoon soaking Homer down with Platinum Frost straight from the bottle. Bubba splashed the dye around like a chef preparing a salad. He crawled underneath the docile buffalo and rubbed it into his belly.

Bubba pulled a garden rake back and forth over the animal's hide to work the coloring in, and Homer came as close to smiling as a buffalo could. The heavy coat that helped the buffalo survive the harshest northern winters for thousands of years was a curse in West Texas. In this country the buffalo spent

131

most of its life shedding out the coat it grew to prepare for a cold spell that would have been little more than an insult to its ancestors. So Bubba's rake lifted great hanks of hair from Homer's body even as it carried the dye to the deepest reaches of his coat.

"Now close your eyes, Homer," Bubba cooed as he grabbed a horn and plied the suds on the animal's immense brow. Homer, who had seen everything that might excite him years ago, behaved like a perfect gentleman. He hadn't received this much attention in one day since the school bus full of third graders stopped for hot dogs and potato chips last October.

When Bubba's arms grew weary, he stepped back to admire his handiwork. He saw a wet, happy buffalo foaming like someone had shaken a keg of beer and turned the spigot on him.

The directions said to let the solution soak in for at least thirty minutes. Bubba was so inspired by the image of a beer-soaked buffalo that he went into the house and started on a six pack. Frank hadn't told him that bleaching a buffalo involved so much hard, physical labor. Still, it felt good, he decided as he worked the kinks out of his back and stretched out on the sofa. A little honest sweat never hurt anyone, no, siree. It had been a good day's work . . .

Two claws dug into Bubba's shoulders, manhandling him back to consciousness. The room spun into view, framing Frank's red, sweat-dappled face.

"Where is he?" Frank demanded.

"Who?" Bubba asked. With Frank thrashing him against the sofa, the word broke up into six or seven syllables like high-speed hiccups.

"Who?" Frank shouted, unsure about which of his brother's stupidities should be the capital offense. "Who? Homer! What did you do with the buffalo?"

Bubba had gathered enough of his senses to wonder if this might be a trick question. "I dyed his hair, just like you told me," he said.

"And where did you put him when you were done?" Frank asked, raising his hands toward the ceiling.

Bubba scrambled off the sofa and peered out the back door. He ran outside and circled the house until he came to the section of pickets that had been flattened on the west side. "Uh oh," he said.

"What?"

"Uh oh."

Frank and Bubba jog-trotted in the direction indicated by the hole in the fence. The clues—pawed-up lawns, a snapped-off sapling, the impression of cloven hooves on the pavement—led them downtown. They found more people lining the broad expanse of Main Street than they'd seen since the last Buford High School homecoming parade.

They followed the gaze of the crowd past the world headquarters of the Fine Fencing Company, past the hardware store and antique shops, past the pharmacy and the Buford Cafe, past the volunteer fire department and the historic marker that commemorated the founding of Buford to the town square where a shaggy, green buffalo was snarfing down grass by the mouthful.

Frank blinked and rubbed his eyes, thinking—hoping—Homer's color was a trick played by the late afternoon sun. But when he looked again, the buffalo was still as green as a ten-dollar bill.

"Why, Mr. Fine, you look like you've seen a ghost."

Frank and Bubba both turned at the familiar sound of Stephanie's voice. She separated herself from the crowd in front of the Fine Fencing Company's world headquarters and tilted her head to get a better look at Bubba. "Your hair's turned white as snow," she said. Then she reached up, felt a curl of her own hair and went on, "Your hair's turned Platinum Frost. And I thought you boys said you were going to dye a buffalo."

Frank looked at Bubba in horror. Bubba looked for his reflection in the window, but found only the image of some clown with white, frizzy hair shooting like fireworks out of his head. He'd been so sloppy applying the potion to Homer that he hadn't realized he was splashing it all over himself.

They realized Stephanie had quit talking and that all these people, their friends and neighbors, were staring at them. Stephanie looked from Bubba to the green buffalo by the court house and back again. "Oh . . ." she said slowly, turning something over in her mind. "I guess maybe buffaloes don't have the same enzymes we do."

Frank and Bubba wanted to disappear. When Sheriff Burbank walked over to Homer and started scribbling in his notebook, they shuffled backwards into the crowd. Stephanie provided a diversion, mumbling, "A buffalo's pH balance might be way off for all I know. I don't think anybody's ever tried this kind of thing before."

Chapter 39
The Wild Horse

On Wednesday morning, Coy took the horses stabled on either side of Money Honey out and let them romp in the big pasture. He and Linnie mucked out their stalls and put a banner over the barn door that said, "See the Wild Horse—25 Cents."

An endless succession of tourists lined the aisle in front of Money's stall. They milled through the adjoining stalls and surrounded the three open sides of her turn-out pen. Hour after hour, people chattered, pointed, laughed and shouted across the way.

At first, Money's nostrils flared. She pinned her ears back and the whites of her eyes shined like spotlights. But the mare had no escape from the commotion and little by little she came to accept it.

Coy and Linnie stacked the coins on the kitchen table that night and counted nearly three hundred dollars.

"It's a crazy old world," Coy mused, "where people will pay more to see a wild horse than a trained one."

But by Saturday morning, when the crowds were about to reach a peak, the wild horse show was history. Money Honey had become so accustomed to the hub-bub that she couldn't fool anyone into thinking hot blood rushed through her veins.

Coy decided she was ready for the next step. He paid a couple of kids to spread the word among all the tourists' children that they could make a quarter by watching a special cutting horse show at two o'clock. When the time came, the little buckaroos stood four deep all the way around the arena.

Coy explained to the kids that they needed to act like a television laugh track to earn their quarters. But instead of laughing, they had to supply sound effects like Money Honey would hear at the Futurity.

"Now when this mare gets her tail down low so she's dragging in the dust, I want you all to shriek just as loud as you can," Coy said. "When she spins around on her back legs and jumps in front of that cow, you have to holler the way your mama tells you not to do at home. And when this horse puts her nose right in that cow's face, you have to whistle and clap. It's real simple."

The kids were so eager, they were ready to cheer just at the thought of being able to let all that pent-up noise out in public.

Coy cut a cow from the herd and let Money show her stuff. Every time the mare made a good move, Linnie let out a shout to cue the kids. Even Coy had to wince at the noise but after a few days' work, Money might have been deaf to the crowd for all the reaction she showed. After each session, Linnie passed out the quarters they'd collected during the wild horse show. By the time they broke even on the deal, Money Honey wouldn't flinch if World War III broke out.

Coy continued to work Doc's Patience first every day with Money Honey and the other young horses tied around the arena where they could watch. One day the most amazing thing happened.

Coy cut a stale old cow out of the herd that just didn't want to move. The cow made a few weak feints that Doc easily contained. She looked at her buddies back in the herd, but she showed little ambition to rejoin them.

Doc blocked her path with his butt low to the ground, half cocked and ready to spring in any direction. His front legs quivered in anticipation, but the cow just blinked and bawled.

And then Doc took Coy by surprise by folding his front legs beneath him in the dirt, as if to tell the cow, "Okay, it's safe now. You can go back to the herd any time you like."

Coy was as surprised as the cow. He shook his head and looked at Linnie in disbelief. He'd never seen anything like this. You couldn't get a cutting horse to do this if you tried. He nudged the gelding with his heels to get him to stand up in case the cow darted, but Doc was intent on the cow and he ignored his rider.

The cow studied the situation, turning it over and over in her bovine mind. Cattle are neither the brightest, nor the most courageous, of God's creatures, but it sure looked like that horse might need a moment to stand up and get its balance before it could move. And a primitive calculator locked in the cow's skull said that it needed only half of that moment to get back to the herd. So, after a long, quivering pause, the cow made a break for it.

Doc sprang up and lunged like a ninja, blocking the cow's path.

Coy put his hand on Doc's neck and broke the silence by whistling in amazement. That made the crowd of kids—to which Coy had been oblivious during Doc's exhibition—erupt with whistles, shouts and applause.

Coy looked at Linnie and they both broke out laughing. The kids had heard about how the cutting horse shows worked at the Double C Ranch and they all wanted quarters.

Coy was in no mood to refuse.

Chapter 40
Yellow Journalism

Howard E. Gray felt like his scoop of the century, the story of Coyote County's white buffalo, had been yanked out from under him by the pushy, big-city media who crowded his territory. He'd researched all the facts and presented them in a clear and enlightening fashion for the Coyoteland Courier's readership before the vultures swooped in from out of town.

He freely admitted that most events which transpired within the borders of Coyote County were of scant interest to those who lived beyond its borders. That admission only strengthened his feeling that he had some proprietary interest in the facts of this story, and that the media invaders had betrayed that interest.

He fully expected to see—at least in some footnote to the national coverage—mention of the fact that he had broken the story. He would have been quick to give such credit, had the roles been reversed. But not a word appeared, not even in the other papers in B.K. Hitchins' Courier empire scattered across Texas.

And, surprisingly, none of the reporters picked up on some of the basic information Howard E. Gray had uncovered, like the succession of ownership of the Double C Ranch site dating back to the 1880s, or the fact that Linnie Cooper could be seen dipping a strip of beef jerky into her cup of black coffee at least a couple times a week at the Buford Cafe. A lot of that stuff just slipped right past the networks and the wire services. You needed an insider's point of view on a story like this.

But Howard E. Gray was never one to hold a grudge, justifiable as it might be. Even after the first wave of publicity, he cheerfully offered his services as a background authority to the outside media for a very minimal fee. When he couldn't find any takers, he approached the Coopers about being their press liaison, and again he was spurned.

These were just the sort of things that drove Howard E. Gray to lambast his television set when the nightly news came on. He bolted to attention in his recliner and scolded the anchorman. He limped around his living room and muttered about the reporter's slipshod journalism, about the way so many important facts were glossed over or missed entirely. It was a national disgrace, he shouted, shaking his fist at the screen. He would be no party to it.

In a way, he identified with the white buffalo of history and legend. Most tribes had seen the white buffalo as the leader of the herd. But the white buffalo's power was its own undoing, for killing such a creature transferred that power to the killer. In some tribes, the white buffalo's remains were allowed to waste in the elements, signifying their purpose in a realm beyond the world through which men moved.

Like that fabled creature, Howard E. Gray stood apart from his peers. His power—the revelation of such basic truths as could be gathered in Coyote County—was usurped by these nomads who preyed on information, and then moved on to the next kill. And in his heart, Howard E. Gray wondered how many times he and his ilk could withstand such assaults before papers like the Courier were herded into extinction.

But some of the ancients also believed that the buffalo that fell in the hunt could reflesh itself and return to the herd of the living. Perhaps that held true for Howard E. Gray and the Coyoteland Courier because now he was on the verge of breaking another story. With his own eyes he had been among the first to glimpse the green buffalo of Coyote County. And he felt certain that when its story was told, the world of B.K. Hitchins' Couriers would never be the same.

Chapter 41
Dining at Caboosi's

Most people see Thanksgiving as the beginning of the holiday season. Cutters, on the other hand, base their calendars on the Futurity when horsemen from all over the country converge on Fort Worth for their day of reckoning.

The Futurity lures so many entrants that horses draw into a two-week series of preliminary rounds that sort the pretenders from the contenders. However these horses are young, and by definition inexperienced. Although a mistake in the early rounds might dash their immediate hopes, many horses that disappear in the Futurity redeem themselves in the coming months and years. Still, most of the talented horses that came to the Futurity in the hands of good trainers survive the elimination rounds to go into the semi-finals.

Stubby Hitchins gave the local gossip columnists a few paragraphs of fodder when he and Tiffany welcomed Coy and Linnie to town by dining at Caboosi's.

"Coy and Linnie Cooper, this is Tiffany," Stubby said as the driver held open the limo's door. "Tiffany, Coy and Linnie Cooper."

"Pleased to meet you, ma'am."

"Hello."

"Hey, you guys."

"Tiffany has a surname, but she won't let us use it," Stubby confided as the waiter handed them their menus.

"It's a career move," Tiffany explained. "Look at Cher and Madonna, for instance. I've done some reading up on this and it all started with a woman called Twiggy."

"What about Socrates?" Stubby interjected, trying to make the kind of sophisticated, light-hearted banter he overheard at the surrounding tables.

"No, I think I'll stick with the lasagna," Tiffany said. "And then I'll diet for a week."

Linnie fanned herself with the menu which had a picture of a branding iron making the impression of an elegant, cursive "C" on the cover. She looked at

Tiffany suspiciously. "Have you ever been to West Texas?" she asked.

"Oh, yes!" she said. Then she felt Stubby's foot rustle her skirt under the table. She knew this was important even though Stubby's legs weren't long enough to give her a good kick in the shin. "I mean, I'm always dreaming about going to West Texas," Tiffany corrected herself. "I guess I'm just a city girl at heart."

"Funny, I never dreamed about it until I went there," Linnie said. "I didn't know there was anything to dream about until I went there."

"Oh." Tiffany smiled and nodded for a moment, then turned abruptly to Stubby. "You were right about these tables," she said.

"How so?" Stubby looked helplessly at his guests.

"That piece of gum I left underneath last time is still here. You'd think they'd clean up more often in a classy joint like this."

With some difficulty, Stubby managed to steer the conversation around to cutting. "So, Coy, do you think Money Honey is ready for this? I hope that mare's not as nervous about it as I am."

"She's a good one," Coy said, fiddling with his silverware. After a moment, he felt Linnie nudge him under the table. "She's been working better than any three-year-old I've ever had. In fact, she's working better than any horse of her age I've ever seen or heard of.

"She knows cows. She's sharp. She's got all the try in the world. But you know, Mr. Hitchins, a fellow might as well be a germ under a microscope for all he can get away with when those judges are looking down at him. It's a tough, tough game. That's why they give the winner so much money."

Stubby leaned over so he could reach Coy's hand to still it. "I'm not worried one bit, Coy. I feel like you've made her a winner already, and that makes me feel like a winner. It's like I was telling Tiffany—"

"Huh-wha?" Tiffany's head swiveled all the way back from outer space to a quiet table at Caboosi's in a split second.

"Didn't I say that Coy probably won't understand it, but I feel like I'm part of that mare just because I brought the pieces together: the horse, the trainer, the bills? None of those things can do you any good without the others.

"That's how all of my businesses work, too, Coy. These business analysts and writers all think I got rich because I'm some kind of genius. But the only thing I know is how to bring the elements together, and then get out of the way."

Chapter 42
Vision Quest

Nothing had been going right since Kenny quit working at the Double C. There weren't many openings in West Texas for up-and-coming cutting horse trainers, but Kenny didn't have the credentials or connections to look for a job closer to Fort Worth, even though opportunities were richer there. So he used Thomas Eagle's place as a home base and drifted from ranch to ranch, filling in for a few days when they were short-handed.

"Nothing wrong with that," Cactus Gordon consoled him at a cutting one Saturday in August. "That's what most fellas did years ago. They'd work until they got crosswise with the foreman or got an itch on their saddle side, and then head off to the next spread. You get yourself exposed to more people and more ideas that way. More cows, too.

"Heck, Kenny, I always thought the best part of cowboying was figuring out what you ought to do in a tight situation. You can't do that if you're always in the same situation."

That sounded fine coming out of Cactus' mouth, but in the day-to-day experience of it, life sure looked harder than it ought to be. Kenny felt truckbound. It seemed like he spent all his time hauling himself to one place or another, and Fresh Freckles wasn't getting the solid work she needed now to be ready for the Futurity.

Kenny helped out an old gas bag of a coot named Dub Carson for a week, down in the corner of Coyote County, until Thomas Eagle told him about one of his clients over by Sweetwater who was in a little bit of a fix. Kenny'd been working from four-thirty in the morning to well past dark and now he had to drive into Buford, borrow himself a trailer, drive back to Carson's place, pick up Freckles, take Freckles to Thomas Eagle's to get her front left shoe re-set, and drive a million miles to this new fellow's place before sun-up.

What Kenny wanted to know about two o'clock that morning was why ranchers didn't locate their places down on the highway so you didn't have to try to figure out some old cowboy's map scratchings in the dark. He wasn't going more than ten miles an hour, fumbling with the flashlight and the map, when he drove into a ditch that was such a perfect fit for the truck that it might have been made in Detroit. He could rev his engine all night long without moving an inch.

The walls of the ditch pressed against both of the doors, so Kenny climbed out the window and went back to check on Freckles in the trailer. It looked like she hadn't taken any harm from being jostled. "Sorry, girl," Kenny said, studying her reaction as he ran his hands along her legs. "It's going to be morning before we get out of this one."

He stood in the trailer a long time, playing the flashlight over the sleek, shiny body of the mare he loved so much. He breathed deeply, hungry for the rich air that has sustained horsemen for generation after generation. He turned the light to a spot on Freckles' neck so he could look at the deep, kind color of her eye. He wished horses could talk; he knew she would share the secret of her contentment if she could.

Kenny climbed back into the pickup, and propped his feet on the dashboard, but he was too exhausted and he had too many things swirling inside his head to sleep. He spent the whole night staring out the dark windshield, wondering what went wrong and what he might do about it. The world didn't seem a whole lot brighter even when the sun transformed the sky.

He was too frustrated to even care about missing his job, or to show much surprise when Thomas Eagle rapped his knuckles on the windshield. "It looks like you missed the road here, Kenny."

"I'm stuck between two worlds," Kenny announced, pulling himself back out of the window.

Thomas stepped back and looked at the truck. "That's right," he said. "Your fenders are stuck in the earth and your wheels are stuck in the air. We'll need some serious horsepower to pull you out of there."

"No, no, no." Kenny waved his arms over his head in frustration. "I'm an Indian and I'm an Anglo so I should feel at home in both worlds. But instead, I don't feel right in either one."

"You're a new person," Thomas said. "You have to find your own way of living."

"But every day for the past six months you've been telling me about these Indian legends, all these things that I don't know what to do with."

"I haven't seen you every day. I haven't even talked with you every day."

"You know what I mean." Kenny walked around in little circles, hunched into himself like he had an itch but he wasn't quite sure where it was. "I've heard you every day even if you haven't said a word. So what do I do? Go live in a tipi somewhere?"

"You can honor the past without living in it. The world is a different place than it was for our ancestors. Maybe it doesn't have room anymore for some of the things they did, but it does have room for their spirit. A man's beliefs, and how deeply he holds them—those are the things that make a good life."

"But I don't know what I believe," Kenny protested. "Nancy McDonald told me the story of the White Buffalo Calf Woman. I understand it, but I don't think that white buffalo at the Double C is going to turn into a woman who teaches our people how to live."

"You can educate a man's head, but you can't educate his soul." Thomas Eagle removed his hat and pointed to the feather in its band. "The feather ties me to the sky which is the world of the spirits," he said. "I wear it on my head to lift my thoughts to higher things."

"Maybe that works for you, but what do I do? Should I get a feather for my hat?"

Thomas leaned against the fender of the mired pickup and sighed. "Remember the vision quest I told you about?"

"You mean when a person goes off and waits for a sign to show him what to do with his life?" As soon as Kenny heard himself say it, the creases began to leave his brow.

Thomas nodded, struggling with the grin that wanted to spread out from the corners of his mouth. "You leave the everyday world for a time," he said. "Then maybe an animal will come to you with a message of your future."

"Like sitting in this truck all night." Kenny rubbed his cheek and neck, feeling his circulation increase.

"Did you see any animals last night?" Thomas asked. "A cow or an owl? Fox? Deer?"

"No." Kenny shook his head, then stopped. "Freckles!"

"What did she tell you?"

"This is so strange." Kenny's eyes widened. "When I checked on her last night, I wished that she could talk. I wanted to know what made her so calm in . . . in the middle of all this." He waved his hand in a circle.

"Have you noticed how many of our people's legends have two characters, a heroic animal and a trickster?" Thomas studied Kenny as he talked. "The eagle and the buffalo, those are heroic creatures. They have noble qualities which inspire us and they offer man gifts or lessons which make our lives better.

"The snake and the coyote, those are usually tricksters. They steal things or pull pranks, but they get what's coming to them in the end.

"Maybe a cutting horse like Freckles is a heroic creature for today's world. We admire her intelligence, her strength, her quickness and her beauty. She brings us happiness, but her skills are also practical things which help us manage the resources we've been blessed with. We are honored to ride her. Like the feather in my hat, she takes our thoughts to higher places."

Kenny wanted to back her out of the trailer, saddle up and ride to the horizon.

"You've got to figure out your own life, Kenny," Thomas went on. "That's what we're all doing here. You can find lessons in anything."

Kenny's grin shrank back just a hair. "Thomas?"

"Yes?"

"Who's the coyote in this story?"

Chapter 43
Video Villains

Stephanie came back to town on the first day of December to give Frank and Bubba their final instructions for the video that would make the Fine Fencing Company a household word. The commercial would show how professional buffalo-nappers or other criminals could beat an ordinary fence faster than it took to tell about it. Then Frank and Bubba would explain how a Brite Buffalo Brand high-security fence, available exclusively from the Fine Fencing Company, "keeps the crooks out, for good."

Stephanie told Frank and Bubba that the production company waited until the Coopers left town for the Futurity so that there would be less disruption to everyday life at the Double C Ranch. And they would be shooting at night, using special infrared cameras.

"Why are we going to shoot at night?" asked Frank, always eager to pick up some tidbit of information that might sound impressive in the re-telling.

"Shadows," Stephanie said, thumbing through the pages on her clipboard.

"But there aren't any shadows at night."

"That's right." She raised her purple-caulked eyes to look at Frank. "You don't want shadows from your hat or trees or anything messing up the picture. They shoot on night film so it looks like daytime, only they don't have to worry about where the sun is, or where the clouds are. All those big Hollywood movies are done like that these days."

"Hm." Frank nodded and went over to Bubba to explain about the shadows.

The script called for Frank and Bubba to play dual roles, first as the buffalo-nappers, and then as the expert fencing technicians who they were in real life. They would install a crime-proof fence, making it safe for buffalo to roam.

"Won't it confuse the audience if we're the bad guys and the good guys?" Frank wondered.

"Oh, no," Tiffany shook her head. "You'll be wearing different clothes." She glanced at the clipboard before going on, "Besides, this will give you extra facial recognition."

145

"Facial recognition?"

"Yeah. You know how you see somebody, but you can't remember where you've seen them before? That's facial recognition. This is all real modern psychology stuff we're using here. They've done all kinds of surveys about these things."

To put Frank and Bubba at ease and make their actions appear more natural, hidden cameras would be used, Stephanie explained. There wouldn't be all of that "cut" and "roll 'em" nonsense they probably expected from watching the midnight movies on television.

"But you'll be there if we have any questions, won't you?" Bubba spoke up.

"Don't worry. I'll see you in the morning." She spread her purple-coated lips in a big smile and sidled over real close to Bubba. "We can watch the raw film together," she breathed. "We'll be the first people in the whole world to see it."

According to plan, Frank and Bubba got into the truck Brite Buffalo Enterprises provided them with to pull the stock trailer that the crooks would use to haul Hope away. They drove to the Double C and left the front gate open for an easy getaway.

"Those camera boys are probably shooting us right now," Frank whispered.

"I don't see them."

"They're hidden so we won't know exactly when they're filming us and when they're not. That Stephanie lady said it's like Santa Claus: he's watching the kids all year."

They followed the curve of the drive to the top pasture where Wanda and Hope mingled with a few of the Double C's other buffalo. Frank stopped outside the fence and cut the lights.

"I can't see them in the dark," Bubba said, squinting at the windshield.

"We don't want any shadows," Frank explained. "Shadows'll screw everything up."

"I mean, I can't see anything in the dark," Bubba protested. "Can I take a flashlight so I don't fall down?"

"Okay, okay, but be careful where you shine it."

Frank gunned the engine and rammed the truck into the fence which gave way like toilet tissue. He left the engine running while they took the rope and the sack of corn out of the pickup bed.

Stephanie had gone over the script with them again and again, insisting that they follow it to the letter. But after she left, Frank had a stroke of genius. He wrote a ransom note, just like a real buffalo-napper would. The only piece of paper he could find which hadn't yet fused into the debris on his desk at the office was the sheet of letterhead from Stephanie's motel in Coyote Town where she'd written the Fine Fencing Company's address the first time she visited them.

Frank had scrawled "Give us $1,000,000 or the white buffalo dies," with his left hand so his writing would be disguised. He pushed the paper onto one of the fence's exposed twists of wire as they moved into the buffalo pasture in search of Hope.

Bubba rattled the corn in the sack and called, "Here, buffalo, come here," as if he were summoning a kitten. He swept the grass with his flashlight.

They'd gone maybe a hundred yards before they could make out a series of dark mounds in the dim light of the stars.

"Okay," Frank said. "She'll be over here with the rest of them."

The men walked slowly forward with their shoulders touching. Their breath rose in ghostly clouds as Bubba panned back and forth with the flashlight. The hulking figures began to stir before them.

"I don't see her," Bubba whispered. "These are all brown buffalo." He let out a low whistle. "They're big, too."

"Over there," Frank pointed to the left. "There's something over there."

Hope blinked and rose to her feet as the light homed in on her. She snorted twice in the cool air.

Bubba rattled the corn and started cooing again, "Here, buffalo. Here, pretty buffalo."

Frank kept letting out the loop in the rope so it would be big enough to fit over Hope's head, which looked much bigger now than he remembered.

Hope shook her head as if she were wearing an uncomfortable hat. She snorted more loudly this time.

"Come here," Bubba murmured. He cradled the light between his side and his elbow as he reached into the sack for a handful of corn. The light slipped and he spilled half the corn into the grass. When he grabbed the light, he dropped the bag.

Frank cursed as he sized the rope. "Shine that light over here so I can see what I'm doing."

Bubba, on his hands and knees, recovered the light. The beam glinted off Bubba's Platinum Frost hair as he fumbled with it.

"Over here," Frank snapped. "Shine it this way."

Bubba turned the light toward Frank, but dropped it instantly. "Holy cow!" he cried as he spun around and ran back the way they came.

Frank looked over his shoulder and saw a massive wall of buffalo building up speed. He dropped the rope and ran a zig-zag course, not quite sure where the truck was against the dark horizon, and too terrified to stop and listen for its engine. The sound of the door slamming sent him in the right direction. A moment later, Bubba drove the pickup to him, the stock trailer fishtailing wildly behind it as the hulking beasts closed in.

Bubba cranked the truck around in a tight circle and threw the passenger door open. Frank dived in on the run. Before Bubba could straighten up, one, two, three heads rammed into the side of the truck with deep and mighty thuds. The pickup wobbled on two wheels and hung in the air for an eternity, just as Frank and Bubba's hearts hung in their throats. Then it toppled onto its side, spinning its wheels in futility as the buffalo, restless and hungry, circled.

Chapter 44
The Futurity

The butterflies came back right on schedule. Their migratory patterns brought them home to the pit of Coy's stomach every time the Futurity started. It was always like this. After a solid year of anticipation and exquisite suspense, Coy just wanted to get the Futurity over with now that the time was at hand.

It seemed like every person he'd ever met in connection with horses came to Fort Worth. But instead of enjoying the renewal of old acquaintances, Coy felt as if he were in a dream, or having one of those near-death experiences where your whole life plays out before you. To the outside world, he looked calm and confident, but to Linnie, Coy's turmoil showed up everywhere, in his meager appetite, constant fidgeting, and the way he read one page of the newspaper over and over.

But just about any other trainer would have gladly traded places with him. Money Honey showed brilliance beyond her years as she cruised through the preliminary rounds and the semi-finals. The mare was good enough that Coy could ride conservatively and still score the points he needed to stay in the game. The way Money Honey could draw an animal to her, the way she would drop her head in front of a cow and swing it like a hypnotist's watch, the way her front legs seemed to be attached to her body by rubber bands, made her a favorite with the crowds.

The only rider who wouldn't have swapped places with Coy was Kenny Rivers. In his first appearance at the Futurity, Kenny embodied the dreams of every young trainer. While most of the seasoned competitors tried for a "safe" ride in the early rounds, Kenny came out of the herd like he was a cutting the last cow on earth. The judges rewarded his guts by giving Fresh Freckles the highest score in both elimination rounds and the semi-finals. Kenny looked like he was poised to sweep away cutting's old guard single-handed.

Kenny wouldn't have traded places with any man on earth. Kenny had always loved his mare, but in the past two months Freckles had blossomed into the world beater he'd seen in her from the start. Even at the Futurity, where the shiny coats of the pampered horses contrasted with the rough, winter hair sprouting from the cattle, Fresh Freckles had a special gloss. Her eyes sparkled with her willingness, her eagerness to do the job she loved.

Sally Harrison, the writer whose stories about the all-time great cutting horses filled Kenny's scrapbook, stopped Kenny and introduced herself after he marked a 222 in the semi-finals.

"Did you have those three cows picked before you rode out there?" asked Sally as Fresh Freckles nuzzled her shoulder.

"Ma'am, I had them picked a year and a half ago." Kenny laughed, finally allowing himself to feel relieved. "I've just been waiting to find them all together in one herd."

Cutters learn humility from the horses and cattle they depend on. "I just wanted to show my horse," they say after a good run, meaning they hope they didn't screw things up too much by being in the saddle.

Kenny felt humble, but he'd lost sight of any distinction between himself and his horse. He and Fresh Freckles moved like a single creature. Now that the countless hours he'd spent honing her skills were about to pay off with more money than Kenny had ever seen at one time, he didn't even think about the cash. Loping his mare at daybreak, rubbing her legs down at nightfall, schooling her in between—those things were the real payoff for Kenny. The Futurity was just a chance to share his mare with his friends. And the audience was ready to scream its lungs out for a good run.

*

A norther blew in the night before the finals and temperatures dropped steadily throughout the day. The predictions of icy roads did nothing to deter the crowds that came for the big event.

Six months ago Coy never would have believed it, but he was actually glad that the coliseum was packed for the finals of the Futurity. Money Honey had seen more whooping and hollering people back at the Double C than the rest of the finalists would encounter in their entire lives. At least nothing was going to distract her from doing her job tonight.

The bad news was that Money Honey drew the very last position in the work order. That meant that most of the cattle that showed any signs of life would have been worked by the time Coy rode into the herd; and a cutter depends on fresh cattle to make a decent score.

Any other time, Coy would have loved to kick back and watch the twenty-one competitors who worked before him. It seemed like all of today's greatest trainers made the finals, and those who didn't took ringside seats to see if they could learn any new tricks. But tonight Coy could hardly stand to be in the coliseum.

He rode over to Linnie in the warm-up area and dismounted. "Here, why don't you lope her?" he said, handing her the reins.

Linnie looked around to see who else was in on the joke. "You want me to ride her into the herd for you, too?" she asked. But when she saw that his nerves had finally transformed his face as well as his habits, she said, "Coy Cooper, what's the matter with you? You haven't let anyone else even touch this mare since August. You don't want to go changing things on her now."

Coy looked trapped. He patted Money Honey on the neck and looked at the whirl of horses warming up at his side. He turned helplessly back to Linnie.

"Take off your hat," she said.

"What?"

"Take off your hat." She reached up and placed her palm on his forehead. "Oh, no, Coy! That's just what I was afraid of!"

"What?" Coy felt his own forehead. "I'm running a fever?"

"You've got stage fright."

"I feel like I'm running a fever." Coy pressed his other hand to his head to confirm his diagnosis.

"That's because you're going to be hot tonight, Coy." She pulled him close and pecked him on the lips. "But you'd better get that horse of yours warmed up."

*

As the seventh rider in the first set of finalists, Kenny broke the Futurity wide open. The crowd, who had heard about his preliminary scores even if they hadn't actually watched the runs, fell silent as Fresh Freckles walked into the arena and tripped the timer.

Even though fashions come and go in cutting, Fresh Freckles was the first horse anyone could remember approaching the herd with a bright red hand print and some primitive yellow shapes drawn on her rump. When Kenny held his head high, it was from pride as much as it was to help him see where the cow he wanted was hiding in the herd.

Cactus Gordon, who was holding herd for Kenny, called out, "That ring-eye you're looking for is over on this side. But don't rush it. She'll wait for you."

As usual, Cactus was right. Kenny rode deep into the herd, quietly driving a stream of cows clear back to the judges' stand. The photographers clutched their equipment and stole glances over their shoulders to see if they had an escape route.

Kenny let the cows trickle back to the herd by ones and twos until the ring-eye was the only one left in front of him. He dropped the reins and Fresh Freckles practically nodded to the cow to make a run for it. The mare sprang to the left to cover the cow's first move, but she popped back in the other direction almost before the cow knew it was going to try to find a path there. Every time the cow thought it found a hole, Fresh Freckles filled it up.

Kenny and Fresh Freckles had the crowd in a frenzy by the time they'd squeezed all the points they were going to get from the ring-eye. They cut two more cows from the herd and worked them with the same skill to earn 224 points by the time the buzzer sounded. A lot of young trainers were thinking about painting designs on their horses' rumps for the spring shows.

*

Coy watched the fresh cattle that came in after the first half of the finalists had finished. He studied their size and weight, their bone structure and coats, their habits and vitality. He got as close as he could and looked into their eyes. He wanted to be on a first-name basis with each of these animals by the time he rode into their midst.

There were some nice rides ahead of him, but nothing came close to Kenny's 224. Coy tried to take deep, calming breaths while he waited for his name to be called. He backed Money Honey and made a couple of tight circles with her to get her mind on the game.

"Just ignore everything but those cows, Coy," Linnie said quietly from behind the rail. "You spend half your life acting like you have blinkers on anyway."

Coy tried to smile. When he turned away Linnie clasped her hands to her chest. She closed her eyes and mouthed words that no cowboy could hear.

It wasn't until Coy heard his name tumble out of the loudspeaker that he realized Cactus wasn't there to hold herd for him. Cactus had such a thorough grasp of the many variables of cutting that some folks reckoned it was worth three or four points just having him down on the arena floor with you when you rode into the herd. Cactus hadn't missed helping Coy at a cutting since a young and naive Coy went to work for him all those years ago.

"Our next contestant is Coy Cooper, riding Money Honey, owned by B.K. Hitchins Jr.," boomed the voice that filled the coliseum.

Panic-stricken, Coy looked at Thomas Eagle, Gary Ryan and Chip Branson, his other three helpers. "Where's Cactus?" he said.

Thomas Eagle shrugged. "I haven't seen him since the cattle change," he said. "I thought he'd be here."

"I did, too." Coy's eyes raced across the warm-up area, searching for his mentor. Adrenaline washed through him. "Okay, okay," he said, filling his lungs with each word.

Coy stopped when he saw Lightning's unmistakable sorrel and white nose poke out of the crowd at the back of the arena. Kenny rode up to him and touched the brim of his hat. "Cactus slipped on the ice and hurt his knee," Kenny said. "So I guess you need a hand here."

"Ice?"

"There's ice outside, Coy," Kenny said through his old poker face. "Most cowboys as old as you have seen ice in the winter time."

"Coy Cooper?" boomed the voice again.

"Is Cactus okay?" Coy stole a quick look at the announcer's stand.

"Fact is, he's going to have a stroke if you don't get out there and show your horse."

Kenny shook his head as he and Thomas, Gary and Chip took their places in the arena. Coy tilted his head back to look for guidance, but all he could see was the ceiling of the coliseum, and his hat fell to the ground.

Sally Harrison handed Coy his hat and said, "I think they're ready for you out there, Coy."

Coy's words stuck in his throat. He cued Money Honey and started on the ride of his life.

Chapter 45
Crime's Payment

Coy and Linnie paid Buck Henderson's son to tend the livestock whenever they were both out of town, so Bo was the first one to find Frank and Bubba stranded in the overturned pickup at the Double C Ranch. The stock trailer had broken away from the pickup and gotten twisted up in a good mess. Frank and Bubba huddled together, shivering in the cab, waiting for the buffalo to leave them alone.

Bo rolled down the window of his truck and cranked up his Ape Linkin tape just as loud as it would go. The buffalo ran like scalded puppies in any direction that would take them out of earshot.

He climbed onto the dented pickup and grinned down at Frank and Bubba. "You guys are in some fix, ain't you?" he said.

Sheriff Burbank let on that he knew certain state and even federal authorities who might share his keen interest in the million-dollar ransom note he found stuck to the fence by Hope's pasture. But he also knew Frank and Bubba, and he believed that of the two things he was sworn to uphold, "order" should sometimes take precedence over "law."

The sheriff's own investigation quickly led him to Fort Worth where he had a long, rambling talk with Tiffany. The young lady's travel expenses to and from Coyote County in recent months had been charged to a no-limit gold card in the name of B.K. Hitchins Jr. In spite of any assurances to the contrary that she'd made to Franklin Fine, Tiffany was not very adept at keeping secrets.

By the time the sheriff had recited the details of Mr. Hitchins' scheme to dupe Frank and Bubba to steal the white buffalo for his private off-shore wild-life preserve, Stubby was wondering where the bottom line was going to fall.

Sheriff Burbank sat down and looked at him level in the eye. He took his badge off his shirt and slipped it into his pocket. "Give them your horse," he said.

"Who?" Stubby asked, confused. "What horse?"

"Give Coy and Linnie your Futurity horse."

"But I love that horse," Stubby protested.

"Not as much as they do," Burbank said, staring hard at Stubby. "You don't have the heart for loving the way they do. You've never had to earn it."

Stubby was flabbergasted. He clasped his hands on the desk and looked at them. "How do you earn something like that?"

"By making a sacrifice." Burbank rose from his chair and looked down at Stubby. "By giving them the horse."

"People who know me say I'm very generous—" Stubby said as the tall man turned toward the door.

Burbank put his hat on and looked back. "One more thing."

"What?"

"Forget about that white buffalo."

Chapter 46
The Big Run

Coy's mood abandoned him when Money Honey entered the herd. Her calmness as she picked a path through the cattle soothed him. The cows themselves seemed like old friends, welcoming him back to the fold. The sharp, familiar smell of the animals, the grip of his chaps, the angle of his boots in the stirrups, all brought him home again. The stirring, mumbling crowd became wallpaper and all Coy could hear was Money Honey's breathing and the advice his helpers called to him.

"That Charolais is a re-work," Kenny said, following Coy's eye to a white cow at the edge of the herd. "Go for the baldy next to it."

Coy looked up at Kenny, and his face must have asked the question for him.

"I tell you it's a re-work," Kenny insisted. "Smitty tried her and it cost him big time twenty minutes ago. You'd know that if you hadn't been wandering around in a daze all night."

Coy cleared his throat and nodded. He let the rest of the cows trickle back to the herd until Kenny's baldy was the only one left.

Money Honey faced off with the cow when he gave her the reins. Her legs quivered in anticipation until the beast shot to the side. She nailed herself in the cow's path, spraying dirt halfway across the arena. Each time the cow moved, the mare matched it, her gleaming mane and tail floating after her in slow motion.

The mare dipped her head and locked eyeballs with the cow. The cow spun around but found Thomas Eagle blocking her escape route. She tried an end run, but Money Honey sprinted in front of her. She tried to feint and dodge, but the mare had seen it all before.

Coy lost himself in the ride, a big, lopsided grin splitting his face. When he'd wrung his points out of the baldy, he came back to the herd for his next cow, feeling the air fill his chest.

"That's about it," Kenny said as Coy scanned the cattle. "There's not a good, fresh cow left in the bunch."

"Take that Charolais," Thomas Eagle called out from behind Coy. "Follow your instincts."

"That's one tough cow," Kenny said. "Didn't you see it?"

"It's a tough business," Thomas said. "You have to do what you think is right."

"Sh!" Coy shook his head at his helpers. He glanced at the clock. He let Money Honey squeeze out a cluster of five cows with the Charolais in front. The mare allowed the Angus and Herefords to drift back to the herd before she planted herself in front of the white cow.

And then time froze for Coy. The Charolais looked at Money Honey and bawled. She raised her tail and jogged a few steps back and forth before she settled in for the night. Thomas and Chip closed in from behind and tried to startle the cow, but they would have needed a moving van to get her off the patch of ground she'd claimed. Money Honey crept up and snorted in the cow's face. Coy whistled and shucked, but the cow might as well have been deaf.

And then Money Honey folded her front legs and went down on her knees, just the way Doc's Patience had done at the Double C that day last summer. And, just like before, the primitive calculator in the cow's head decided that it could sneak back to the herd before this horse could regain its feet.

Wrong.

Money Honey's powerful haunches catapulted her in front of the cow so that her hooves pushed up a curtain of dirt. The cameras' flashes blinded Coy, but Money Honey locked on to her quarry and thrived on the game. When the buzzer sounded, Coy couldn't hear it for the crowd. He didn't pull the mare back until he saw Kenny pointing to his watch and mouthing, "Time!"

Linnie practically pulled Coy off the mare when he got to the back of the arena. "I don't know who to kiss first," she shouted, "You or Money Honey."

"Well, she's more patient than I am," Coy confessed.

Linnie pulled away from their kiss when the crowd's roar signaled a 226 on the scoreboard.

Chapter 47
Where Buffalo Roam

Even B.K. Hitchins Sr., who spent his entire life grousing about the wasteland he saw when he looked at West Texas, had to make an exception once a year.

Wildflowers spring forth as a seductive counterpoint to the irresistible green of the earth and the sky's overarching blue. The air strikes a precarious balance between too hot and too cold. The breeze through the mesquite carries the scent of life and the song of renewal, a song more ancient than words.

Spring transforms the lonely stretches of West Texas into something all the more beautiful for its bigness. It's a time that stirred the buffalo when buffalo ruled the land.

"On days like this you can see why my people felt that the animals and trees and plants, even the rocks, had a spirit," Kenny told Coy and Linnie as they drove to the Double Mountain River State Park. "Doesn't it seem like everything is sharing a message that it wants us to understand?"

Coy never found out why Mr. Hitchins signed Money Honey's papers over to him, but he counted his blessings each morning. Any barriers the future might have held fell away when you had a horse—a work of art—like that in your barn.

"It's like all those people who came out to your ranch to see the white buffalo," Kenny went on. "You cussed them right through coffee time, but they helped you win the Futurity."

"I reckon a few of them cussed me, too," Coy laughed.

"The thing is, you didn't know it, and they didn't know it, but you were all part of something big, something exciting.

"I tell you what, though," Kenny added, slapping the dashboard, "it's easier to figure things out after they happen. Maybe if I listen to my horse well enough, she'll let me know what's going on while it's going on!"

Coy had been so intent on the Futurity that he didn't let himself take stock of the Double C until after Christmas. They'd tried to take good care of Hope, but the ranch had become too much like a sideshow. She needed to find her place in the real world, a world of buffalo and open spaces, not cameras and tourists.

Kenny ran his fingers through the white buffalo's thick winter coat as they took her off the trailer. "I'm going to miss you, girl," he said.

Coy thought of all the aggravation and turmoil that had come along with Hope, but he wasn't lying when he said, "I guess I am, too."

Linnie took the paperwork from the ranger and said, "I feel like she's my baby. You'll take good care of her here, won't you?"

"She'll feel like she was born here," he said. "Buffalo love company more than anything. Our herd will take her right away."

"I'm so happy and so sad, all at the same time," Linnie said. "I hope we're doing the right thing."

Coy pulled her close to him, but he didn't know what words would reassure her.

Kenny slapped Hope's rump to send her off toward the brown tufts that ambled along the river in the slant of early sunlight. "I don't guess we'll ever see anything like the old buffalo days again," he said. "But we've got to hold onto as much as we can so we don't forget them.

"Thomas Eagle and Cactus sat me down for a long talk just before the Futurity. Cactus said old-time cowboys are gone, but our cutting horses keep a part of them alive; the most important part, their spirit. You just have to climb in the saddle to see that.

"Thomas said it's the same thing with the buffalo. They'll never be the way they used to be in the old days, but we can do our best to see them through in the kind of world we've made for them and for us now."

They watched the sun play on the fringes of Hope's pure white coat, embroidering it with gold. As she walked into the valley to join her new herd, Coy's eyes wandered off to the horizon.

He turned to Linnie and said, "No fences."

To find out about more books about cutting horses, and more novels by Alan Gold, visit fifthleg.com.

www.ingramcontent.com/pod-product-compliance
Lightning Source LLC
Chambersburg PA
CBHW020621250626
47154CB00004B/1611